ZAIN

EVIE MONROE

Copyright and Disclaimer

This book is a work of fiction. The names, characters, places and incidents are products of the writer's imagination and have been used fictitiously and are not to be construed as real. Any resemblance to persons, living or dead, actual events, locales or organizations is entirely coincidental.

Copyright © 2019 Book Boyfriends Publishing

Table of Contents

Zain

Steel Cobras MC Book 6

By Evie Monroe

Chapter One

Zain

The Hell's Fury—our rival gang and the biggest thorn in our side—was out for blood. And I was the start of it all.

Once again, the Steel Cobras sat around church mulling over the hot topic of conversation: how the hell we were going to put an end to the Fury's shitstorm once and for all. It had been going on for three years for fucks sake.

I glanced at my brothers. Each one of them officers in the best motorcycle club in Aveline Bay. Hell, the whole West Coast. They all looked like they'd aged decades in the three years since I'd met them.

Being part of the Steel Cobras was the best thing that'd ever happened to me. I knew I wanted to be in a motorcycle club from the time I was about seven or eight years old. When all of the other kids were playing sports in the recess yard of my private school, I would sit and watch this big dude fixing up his bike in the row houses outside the playground.

Big, jacked dude with tattoos up and down his arms and a *fuck you* attitude. Even the biggest bullies respected that dude. And he had the sweetest ride. A Harley he spent most of the day polishing up so that the chrome sparkled like diamonds.

Sometimes at recess, a pretty lady would come and jump on the back of the bike with him and they'd tear off to wherever.

In school, I never wanted to be an astronaut or a lawyer or a doctor like the other kids. No, I wanted to be that guy—the fucking biggest badass I'd ever seen.

The problem was, I was so hyped up on becoming that guy, I didn't care how I got there. And I fell in with some bad dudes.

The Hell's Fury.

No bigger bunch of assholes had ever existed.

And now here we were, trying to put out a fire I'd ignited three years ago when I'd jumped ship from Hell's Fury to the motherfuckin' Steel Cobras.

I wasn't far off from the guy I admired as a kid.

I was jacked.

I had the tattoos.

I had the Harley.

I had the same *fuck you* attitude.

The only thing I didn't have was the pretty lady. Although, I did have a selection of blondes, and brunettes, and red-heads, one for every day of the month. And I liked that a hell of a lot better.

So I'd gotten the life I'd dreamed of. The life most of the men around this table had dreamed of, too. They'd all had similar ideas of becoming bad-asses, or else they wouldn't have been here.

If only I hadn't gone straight to the Cobras and hadn't messed with the Hell's Fury to begin with. Then my life would have been perfect. But I was stupid back in the day.

That little incident, about three years ago, had started this whole feud.

Slowly, it'd been building, and now it had come to a head.

Three years. Three years of fighting back-and-forth, of watching all the guys I called my brothers suffer, walking around with eyes on the backs of their heads.

We sat around the table at the clubhouse that evening, tense. It'd been a long night, with all of us agreeing we needed to take out the Fury, but none of us keen on waiting for the right time to do that.

So far, there'd been battles here and there. They'd kidnapped our girls, threatened us, shot at us, tried to destroy our clubhouse. But when they killed Joel, the little brother of Hart's girl, they went too far. Way too far.

The all-out war was coming. It was just a question of when.

And every fucking time something like this happened, every time the Fury drew Cobra blood, I was reminded that I was the start of it all.

I was the reason Joel was dead.

I was the reason Jet had taken a bullet in the stomach.

I was the reason several of the Cobra's girls were afraid to go out at night.

I was the reason the other Cobras had to watch their backs.

Hart, our Secretary and tech guy, ran both hands through his hair and growled. The night was getting to him, the hour, his anger over what they'd done.

"It's time," he announced, pounding the table. "Joel was the last straw. They killed him purely out of spite. We need to avenge him. I want to tell Charlotte we're going to take care of it, for her brother. She's scared to death they'll come after me now or her."

Nix shook his head in disgust. "Liv is, too. She keeps wondering what'll happen when she has our baby."

All the guys nodded to signal they were ready.

But I couldn't say a word.

I hated the Fury as much, if not more, than all of them, but I was the only one of them without a girl. My reasons for getting rid of the Fury were my own. They'd given me shit since the early days when I'd been a prospect with them. And it only got worse when I defected to the Cobras.

It was a good thing I could hold my own in a fistfight. But having a good right hook could only get me so far. I lived every day knowing I was Public Enemy Number One in their eyes. They made it no secret that they wanted me dead. Executing Joel in cold blood for the same crime showed me they weren't bluffing.

They were sending me a message, one I read loud and clear. *You're next*.

But as much as I wanted them gone, I didn't want any more Cobra blood spilled because of a fire I'd struck the match to start.

"It's gonna get worse and worse for us until we take them out," said Nix, the Vice President of the club. "We keep going over this. Same shit, different day."

Our president, Cullen, took a swig of his beer and stroked his beard. "Look. If it was just a matter of pressing a button and dropping a bomb on the Fury, I'd be for it. But the fact remains, they're a much bigger club than the Cobras. They have clubs and clubhouses everywhere, and we never know where they're gonna be. Every time we see them, they've got more guys. We can't just walk in there and take them out without some serious casualties."

Hart scowled. "Yeah, but you saw what they did to Joel. We should rip their fucking hearts out by hand for that."

Jetson, our Sargent at Arms and the baby of the group, stirred in his seat. He was a little pissant most of the time, saying shit that usually had us wanting to kick his ass. But he'd gotten a lot better since he'd taken that bullet in the stomach and started shacking up with Nora, that hot surgeon of his. "They're asking for it," he said, sounding wise for once in his life.

"Sure they are. Because they know that if they keep provoking us, we'll fly off the handle and do stupid shit. We do something stupid like attack them with the numbers they have, they can go and pick us off one by one." Cullen said.

"What the fuck? You were there! They blew the kid's brains out and laughed about it," Hart ground out, shooting eye daggers at Cullen. I was sure he'd gotten more than an earful from Charlotte, his girl and Joel's older sister. "They did that out of spite for us. We can't just let them walk all over us."

It'd been a fucking nightmare. The nineteen-year-old kid made the mistake of becoming a prospect for the Fury, just as I had. We'd caught him taking pot shots at Nix and Jet, learned that he was just a naïve, scared little kid, and eventually we all came to like the guy and offered to make him a prospect. He liked us too, decided to bolt from the Fury and gave us some fresh intel on their recent operations. And because we liked him?

He got a bullet in his head for that trouble. They executed him right in front of us.

"It's no secret the Hell's Fury is a bad club. The kid knew what he was getting into."

Hart slammed his fists down on the table. "This is bullshit!"

Cullen didn't flinch. He leaned back and checked out his fingernails, unimpressed by the show of testosterone.

I could've set the record straight on that one. Not everyone was as well informed as Cullen was. Bad meant different things to different people. I'd gotten in with the Fury because I wanted to be part of the biggest, baddest club in Aveline Bay. I hadn't done any research, just acted on what I'd heard on the news. I'd thought the Fury was it.

By the time I'd learned I was wrong, that the Fury were bad as in total assholes, I was in too deep to simply back out and say I'd made a mistake.

When you're accepted into the Fury? You're Fury for life, however long that might be. And if you try to leave? Your life expectancy just got a hell of a lot shorter.

Cullen reached for his pack of cigarettes and tapped one out, then put it back. He'd been trying to quit but had been doing a shitty job of it. "You give me a good way we can get to them without killing ourselves in the process, and maybe I'll bite. But they have twice as many men as we have. I'm not leading the Cobras into a bloodbath."

Our president did have a point. He hated the Fury as much as the next guy, but we didn't have the numbers to launch into a full attack.

"So what?" Jet put his elbows on the table and winced a little. "We just sit back and do nothing? That's fucked."

"You have any better ideas, put them on the table. But yeah. Right now, there's nothing we can do," Cullen said.

The room erupted, men shouting and trying to be the loudest in the room. Hart pushed away from the table and stalked back and forth, raking his hands through his hair. All talk, no listening. My head pounded.

Cullen banged his fist on the table and quieted everyone down. He looked at me, the only person who hadn't said a word. "Zain. It's clear how all these guys feel. But you've been too quiet. What about you? What do you think?"

Since I'd once been a prospect for the Fury, Cullen usually turned to me for advice. Sure, I knew stuff about them, but I wasn't sure I had anything new to help us now.

"We may have taken Slade out, but now they've got Scar. Bad dude, man. He's just as bad, if not worse than Slade. Whatever Joel told us about them falling apart without a leader ain't gonna be in effect anymore. It's a risk," I said.

Cullen nodded, but the rest of the guys? That wasn't the answer they wanted to hear. Hart especially. "I don't fucking care," he said, drumming his hands on the table. "If we don't do something about them now, I'm going to have to take Charlie out of here. She can't live this way. She wants to leave Aveline anyway, knowing what happened to her little brother."

Jet nodded. "Yeah. Nora's flipping out. She's been talking about transferring to another hospital, just to get away from this Fury bullshit."

Nix, his older brother, added, "I have to escort Liv to her dance rehearsals. No way in hell am I letting her go by herself. She's too little to protect herself against those assholes."

Drake, our treasurer, tucked his long hair behind his ear. He didn't say anything at first, but he didn't have to. His girl Cait and her mother, Roxanne were daughter and wife of Slade, the Fury's former president. Ever since we'd offed Slade, we'd had his family in hiding. Months, now. It had to have been getting old for him.

Drake added, "Cait thinks that the more we wait, the weaker we look and the stronger they'll get. They've been prospecting as far as San Fran. For Aveline Bay. Fuckers are cold blooded killers."

Cullen nodded slowly. He was probably thinking of his girl, Grace, and his daughter. They all had a lot riding on this war with the Fury.

I didn't have anyone but myself. The only thing I felt was responsible for the whole shitty affair. Countless lives were either over or in danger because of my one stupid move.

After all, if I hadn't defected, it was possible that the two clubs could've coexisted in Aveline Bay, California.

Not now. And it'd just gotten worse over the years.

We had to do something. I'd take care of it myself, but I'd already caused enough shit for these guys. I didn't want to be the one that ended up getting all of them killed.

So I'd come in here knowing I wouldn't talk unless I had to.

Everyone restless, they started throwing out their opinions again. The shouting rose to a head, loud enough that I couldn't take it anymore. It felt like someone was drilling into my goddamn brain with a corkscrew. This was fucking petty drama, which I hated.

I put up my hands. "Fuck this. Y'all are driving me insane. I'm heading out." I pushed away from my chair as they all turned to stare at me. Grabbing my helmet, I said, "Let me all know what you decide. I'm in, either way."

I strode to the door, flung it open, and went out to my bike, leaving them staring after me. They didn't get it. I felt like shit. They were my brothers and seeing them go through this felt like a fucking cement block tied around my neck.

ZAIN

Because I'd started the whole damn thing, so I didn't deserve a vote.

EVIE MONROE

Chapter Two

Sasha

"Where are you, *solnyshka?*"

Even though it was only a voicemail, the voice of my ex-husband nearly made my skin crawl.

I dropped the phone on my desk with a clatter that made everyone in the office look up.

Glancing at the clock, my pulse skittered. 5:05.

I grabbed my handbag and left the pile of papers for the Wilson insurance fraud case scattered on my desk. I'd clean it up tomorrow.

I was late. Only five minutes late, now, but Viktor was the kind of man who did not like to be kept waiting.

I pushed in my chair and headed for the door.

As I waved goodbye to the interns and a few of the other friendlier faces in the office, my co-worker,

Marina, called loudly, "Look who's checking out early. Bye Sasha!"

I frowned at her as I pulled my jacket over my blouse and hefted my folio bag onto my shoulder. "It's not early."

"Well, for some people, it might not be," she said with a hint of superiority, fluffing her curly black locks.

"I understand, Marina. But I've got to pick up Alena."

"Or so you say."

I frowned. "What is that supposed to mean?"

She huffed like it wasn't a good enough excuse and stepped over to her cubicle.

I suppressed the urge to curse under my breath. Marina Lopez clearly wanted the promotion to head paralegal so much she was salivating for it. Happily married to a doctor with no children, she didn't know the struggle I went through, day after day. She was always making me look bad in front of my boss, Mr. Robert Simms, the most important half of Simms and

Simms, the downtown law firm headed by him and his younger brother.

As I headed for the door, my heels clicking too loudly on the hardwood floor, I ventured a look in Robert Simms' office. Luckily, he was busy on the telephone, his chair turned away from the door, so I made it out of the office without him seeing me slip past him.

I didn't dare believe I was so lucky as to have not gotten caught. Undoubtedly, Marina would fill him in the second he hung up the phone.

As I pressed the DOWN button for the elevator, Sarah Chin stopped me in the hall. "You're going? So soon?"

I rolled my eyes. "Please don't, Sarah. I already got a guilt trip from Marina."

She checked her phone and patted my arm. "Oh. I didn't realize what time it is. I didn't mean to imply anything. I know you have to get Alena."

I sighed. "Thanks, Sarah."

She looked around to make sure we were alone and leaned in. "And don't worry about Marina. That girl's a witch with a B. You're fine. We were almost done here, anyway. The Wilson case will be fine. I'll handle everything."

Sarah was a true star. She was sweet, kind, dedicated, a true team player. I smiled at her as the elevator bell dinged above me and the doors slid open. I stepped inside. "Thank you so much, Sarah. I owe you for this."

"No you don't!" Sarah called as the doors slid shut. "Have a good weekend!"

Sarah had been my ally at Simms & Simms since I started there a year ago, after my divorce was final. My only ally. I loved the job, and the Simms brothers always complimented my work. What I loved most about working was making my own money and having my independence.

I'd had enough of being under a man's thumb. Never again.

ZAIN

Over my dead body.

I let out a big sigh as I studied my reflection in the mirror of the elevator doors. I looked the part. Cheap—but professional—skirt. Sweater. High heels. My dark hair was pulled back in a professional braid. Young, but not too young. That promotion would've been more money. A better life for Alena and me.

But I still didn't speak English perfectly despite taking a monthly class at the Community College. I'd tried to soften my accent, to no avail. And sometimes it was so thick, people didn't understand me. I still had trouble with the *w* sound; I always pronounced it as a *v*. Sarah thought it was sexy, but I just wanted to sound like everybody else.

And Marina had been at Simms & Simms longer than I had been. The new position would likely mean even longer hours and I wasn't sure I could do that. Yes, I wanted a better life for Alena, but not if it meant spending less time with her. Regardless of the guilt trips Viktor threw on me, I was a mom to my daughter first and a paralegal second.

Of course, Marina had plenty of extra hours to spend with the Simms brothers, trying to show her dedication and prove herself worthy of the new Senior Paralegal position the law firm was opening up in the next month.

I didn't mind that, but what I did mind was her trying to make the rest of us look bad so that she could look better.

I cringed at the thought of Marina getting the job. Almost anyone else in the firm would be a better choice. If I had to report to Marina, with her pinched scowl, navy suits and her thousand-dollar high heels? I'd probably end up hating my life and wanting to jump off a short pier. She always made me feel like I was doing something wrong.

Speaking of always making me feel like I was doing something wrong . . .

Viktor. I checked the time on my phone. Oh, he was going to give me so much crap when I got to his house. I could almost feel his impatience growing, even from miles away. I needed to hurry.

When I reached the lobby, I kicked off my heels, took them in my hands, and sprinted barefoot to my car.

As I slid into the driver's seat, my phone rang again. I looked at the display and groaned. Viktor, of course. He was probably steaming. I knew better than to not answer. Breathing hard and bracing myself, I lifted the phone to my ear. "I'm on my way now. I had to stay late at work."

His voice was hard. "*Solnyshka,* what did I tell you?"

Oh, he'd told me plenty of things that were burned into my head. Many were buried so deep in my brain that it'd taken me years to escape him. Even now when I drifted off to sleep his voice sometimes played in my mind: *Watch Alena, be careful with Americans, they can be untrustworthy. Don't answer the door for people you don't know. How many times to I have to tell you to keep your phone charged at all times?*

When we first married, I'd been so in love that I couldn't possibly dream of him hurting or undermining me. Then I got pregnant and was alone in this new country with no money, no means of supporting myself. I could barely speak English.

He gradually engrained into my head that I needed him; that I wouldn't survive without him.

So many things that still made me doubt myself.

I turned the key in the ignition. "I know," I said, "but I couldn't take myself away from my job because I had an important case. I'm stopping at the daycare right now, and I'll be at your apartment in fifteen minutes."

He let out his typical hmph. I knew it so well. Nothing I ever did was good enough for him.

"If you wanted her so badly, Viktor, you know that you could've picked her up from daycare."

His voice was a low grumble. "I'm too busy."

And I'm not? I wanted to yell at him, but I bit my tongue. I'd see him in fifteen minutes, and I never wanted Alena to see any hint of bad feelings between us. "All right," I said, doing my best to hide my irritation. "I'm doing the best I can. I had an important case to prepare for."

He lowered his voice and spoke in Russian, something he only did when he was being absolutely serious. I should've known he wouldn't care about my job. He wouldn't even care if I were saving the free world from total destruction. He said, "You're not following your end of the deal. This is the third time this month."

"Yes, I know, but—"

"If this continues, I'll have no choice but to go back to the judge and ask for full custody."

The threat shook me to my core. I couldn't let that happen. Alena was the bright spot of my life. At four, she was my closest family. And it wasn't because he desperately missed Alena and wanted to spend more time with her. He knew that by threatening to take Alena away from me, he'd scare me into submission. It worked.

"Please, Viktor, I—"

"—Just get here." And he ended the call.

I put the phone down in the center console and swallowed. One thing I'd learned from the six years I'd known Viktor was that he often carried through with his threats. Big and imposing, he made men cower with a simple glare of his steel-gray eyes.

If only I'd been that afraid of him when we'd met in Moscow. Maybe then, I could've run in the other direction and this never would've happened.

Now, we were tied to each other. Having his child only made sure his hold on me would last forever.

The Little Learners Daycare was right down the street from my office, so I drove there quickly and parked out front. As I passed the colorful murals and artwork of the various children in the Pre-K room, I heard a bright voice call, "Mommy!"

That was always the absolute best part of my day.

I crouched as a little dark-haired dynamo rushed me, wrapping her little arms around my waist in an enthusiastic hug that nearly knocked me off my feet.

She pressed her cheek into my belly and chirped, "I'm so happy!"

I tugged on one of her pigtails. "And why is that?"

"Blaire said I'm the best kickballer in the class. And I made a maraca out of beans and a cup. You make music with it. And I could color it any way I liked so I drew a picture of you and me. Want to see?" Her mouth ran like a motor.

I nodded, my bad mood melting away as I listened to her infectious giggle. "Of course!"

She took my hand and dragged me to the window. A number of art projects covered the windowsill, drying in the sun. She pointed her picture out to me, and I had to laugh. She'd given me a big head and strange hair that went down to my toes, but we both had such huge smiles.

She never painted Viktor in any of her artwork. She always cried whenever I had to send her there. Something told me that Viktor was far too busy with his business dealings to take Alena out for ice cream or mini golf, like I was fond of doing, whenever I could scrape some extra cash together.

He loved her, yes. Loved me, too. But he had trouble expressing that. He'd had a very harsh upbringing in Russia, with parents who were very strict, and he didn't know how to show love. And Alena and I—his only family in this country—were afterthoughts. Second to his successful business ventures, whatever they were. I didn't even attempt to understand. And the main reason Viktor wanted custody of Alena was to get back at me for leaving him.

I knew that.

I wished we could be civil, for Alena's sake. I'd tried to be. But Viktor wasn't having any of that. He wanted to get in his digs, wherever he could, with the hope that eventually I might believe that I wasn't good enough to make it on my own and come crawling back to him.

"It's beautiful, *myshka*," I said to her, nuzzling her soft cheek with my nose as I crouched next to her. "But don't touch. Let it stay and dry and you can bring it home next time. Come, let's get your bag and go."

She ran to her cubbyhole, where she pulled out her pink princess backpack and her Elsa jacket. We said thank you and goodbye to her teachers chatted happily as I guided to my car. I strapped Alena into her booster seat and took a breath before my next task.

"Now," I said gently, looking into her big brown eyes. "You know you're going to daddy's."

She nodded, her smile fading to a pout. "I wish I didn't have to go, Mommy."

I twirled one of her pigtails around my finger. "It'll be okay. It's only for two days. Two sleeps, tonight and tomorrow night. I'll pick you up Sunday afternoon. And Daddy is excited to see you. He just called me, saying he couldn't wait for all the fun things you'll be doing."

She eyed me doubtfully. Even she seemed to know that I was lying.

"Daddy is not so bad!" I said brightly. "You told me last time he gave you your favorite for dinner. Hot dogs."

"His housekeeper did that. He's always working." She stuck her bottom lip out in a pout that crushed my heart.

"Yes. Well, you tell him you want some time with him. He loves you. He'll listen to you," I offered.

When I met Viktor, he had a big, soft heart. I could bat my big brown eyes and make him do anything for me. He'd dazzle me with his warmth and smile and murmur, "You bewitch me with your eyes, and I will do whatever you want."

Not anymore. But Alena had a better chance. Our gorgeous little temptress already had an attitude. She'd catch Viktor with one of her delicious smiles, and I'd see him melt just as I do. In another ten years, we'd be in trouble.

I kissed her forehead and closed the door, then got into the driver's seat, put on her favorite CD of kid's songs, and drove north, to the complex where Viktor lived.

As I did, I kept checking the rear-view mirror and smiling at Alena's beautiful, angelic face. She had my eyes, and they lit up as we drove, reflecting everything she saw as she peered out the window. It was hard to believe that something so beautiful could have come from something that had soured so badly.

If only we could've made it work. That was all I wanted when I came to this country. Family. Happiness. Love. Stability.

Was it too much to ask?

Viktor's condominium complex was not far from the daycare. He lived in an enormous condo in a wealthy section of town. Alena and I lived in a small one-room studio over a Chinese restaurant. With the alimony payments I received, I couldn't afford anything else. I didn't mind it, though. I liked the simple life. It was just Alena and me and together we were happy.

Alena didn't seem to care that at her father's house she had an enormous bedroom with a canopy and all the stuffed animals she could want. He also had a game room with an air hockey table and a massive television. She still liked my place better. She dragged her feet as I took her little hand and led her to his front door.

"Come, *myshka,*" I said, squeezing her hand. "You'll have fun."

"I'd have more fun with you," she pouted, as I took her princess backpack and helped her up the stairs.

The door of his condominium flew open as we approached. My ex-husband stood there, his stocky form filling the entire width of the doorway. I looked up to see his big steely eyes glowering at me.

Alena hid behind me. I stepped aside and she shyly said, "Hi, Daddy."

Eyes never leaving mine, he said, sternly, "Hello, Alena. Please go inside. Daddy needs to speak to your mother."

Gnawing on her lip, she nodded and looked up at me. I crouched down and gave her a big hug and a kiss on the cheek. "Be a good girl and do as your daddy says, all right? Remember. I'll be here to pick you up on Sunday afternoon. Okay?"

She nodded and hugged me tighter. I had to pry her little arms away, which tugged on my heartstrings.

When she ran into the house, I cringed, bracing myself for the onslaught.

Viktor stepped outside, his face grave. He was a handsome man, with dark hair cut in a severe, military way and steely eyes, but he'd lost all that boyish, fun-loving charm he'd had when we'd met in Moscow. We used to laugh. He used to smile. Now, he was so intense, always frowning, never lighthearted in the least. No wonder Alena was scared of him. He scared me, too sometimes, especially when he looked at me the way he was looking at me now. Like I'd failed him, done something wrong.

"Are you trying to turn her against me?" he hissed out, eyes narrowed.

ESNTML

"What? No, of course—"

He clamped a hand over my arm and pulled me toward him. Never hard enough to bruise, but always hard enough to get me to fall in line and fear him. "If I hear you are, I will not be happy, Sasha. You know I never say anything against you to her."

I sighed. I got the feeling he never said anything at all to her, since he was too busy working. "I know. I don't. You could smile at her and spend time with her. Maybe she wouldn't be so scared to come here. I am trying to keep everything between us positive, for Alena's sake."

"If you were doing this for Alena's sake, then you and I should still be together," he grumbled. "A child should have her mother and father."

"You know we can't be," I mumbled. It was the same argument every time we got together. "We fought too much when I was here."

"No."

"*Yes*. You can't doubt it. You may think you want me back, but you know things were worse when we were married."

He eyed my skirt and sweater, then reached out and touched the collar. "And this is you? Working for a living? You look ridiculous, like you're play-acting. I gave you everything so that you wouldn't have to work. So you could stay at home and be a real mother to our daughter."

"I *am* a real mother to her, Viktor. Just because I work doesn't mean I'm abandoning her. And I love my career. I'm setting a good example for her, whether or not you think so."

He gave me a doubtful look. "I don't like it. Dropping her off with strangers every day? That's a good example?"

"They're not strangers at Little Learners. Her teacher is wonderful. And she loves it there. She's learning so much and she has so many friends."

He grumbled what sounded like, *Vot eto pizdets*, and let go of my arm. *Life is fucking me.* Then he kissed me lightly on the temple. *"Ya liublyoo tibya, solnyshka."*

I love you, sunshine.

I looked up at him, dangerously close to cracking. Growing up, all I'd wanted in my life was the family: me, my husband, and my children. When Viktor offered it to me, I ran blindly into marriage without thinking. And it became a nightmare.

He waited for me to reply with the same, but instead, I said, "Please watch over Alena. I know you're busy but try to give her some of your time."

He frowned. "Of, course I will."

"Dasvidaniya, Viktor." *Goodbye.* I wrenched myself away from him and hurried to my car.

By the time I buckled my seatbelt, I was shaking. I pressed my forehead against the steering wheel and tried to collect myself.

How could I say I loved him? Yes, I cared about him, but he wanted a good little puppet to keep home, fat and pregnant while he went off, living his life. He didn't want a wife. He wanted a servant.

Oh, how I hated these meetings with Viktor. It was always the same. Half of the time he was trying to control me, the other half he was trying to woo me back. He never seemed to understand it was his try controlling behavior that had made me leave in the first place.

I'd fought for two years to get up the courage and strength to leave. I would never go back to him, ever.

When I pulled out of the parking lot, I felt a little better. For the first time in weeks, I'd have a whole weekend to myself.

As relief washed over me, I started reeling through the possibilities. I could read a book. Or fix up the house. Or practice some of my English lessons.

But when I looked up and saw the sign for a place called The Wall, I had a better idea.

EVIE MONROE

I hadn't had a drink in over a year. Not since I celebrated the finalization of my divorce from Viktor. And that was just a simple glass of wine that my lawyer had given me.

I wanted something more.

I slowed and put on my blinker, then turned into the full parking lot. When I cut the engine, I pulled my hair out of the braid, fluffed it, and shrugged out of my blazer.

Right now, I could use something to get this weekend started and calm myself down. Vodka, neat.

Maybe a double.

Chapter Three

Zain

I rode my bike back toward my place. As I headed up the highway, I thought about church. How the hell did we get ourselves into such a fucking tight spot?

Nix would say it'd started when we lifted that car outside the country club. The Fury worked with a guy named Anderson who'd fucked with them. They kidnapped his daughter, Liv, and tossed her in the back of a Mercedes S-Class. So instead of Anderson getting the warning message from the Fury, we'd found her when we popped the trunk. Then Nix and Liv got together, and fell in love, but not before pissing the Fury off royally.

Cullen would probably say it was Grace. He'd been so intent on protecting his girl and daughter, he'd gone overboard and pissed off a bunch of Fury with some seriously bad attitude. That had resulted in an all-out gunfight.

Drake would've said it was Cait, the Fury president's daughter. We'd had to step in when it turn out that her dear old dad, Slade, was abusing her. We wound up killing Slade in that fight.

I'd bet Jet would've blamed it on Nora. He'd fallen for Nora after he got a gunshot to the stomach in the fight. He landed in her hands as the surgeon who fixed him up. But he'd gotten the Fury plenty pissed off when they came looking for him. Jet was always going around looking for trouble. He loved egging the Fury on.

And Hart would've said it started just a little while ago, with Charlotte and Joel, her little brother. We nabbed Joel during the fight working as a Fury prospect, but we made him our friend. And because of his allegiance to us, the Fury took him out. Right in front of our eyes. Talk about sending a message.

Yeah, Fury had good reasons to start more shit, in addition to the fact that we'd begun to cut into their business.

But really, the start of it all? It was me.

I was twenty-six when my parents died. At that point, I was the biggest fuck-up you could imagine.

I started doing heroin when I was a sophomore in high school, at a party with a bunch of my rich asshole friends. We did it casually back then, only on weekends, so no one really knew. After leaving high school, I went to college for a semester, but then I dropped out. I'd started about fifteen different career training programs, for everything from plumbing to carpet laying. I'd gotten kicked out of each one because I was high. By then, I'd progressed to using every day.

I couldn't get my shit together. At twenty-six, I was still living in my parents' basement, still penniless, putting every single dollar I got toward drugs. I hung out with some really bad people.

I kept telling myself that it would never be too late to turn things around. Eventually, I'd get out of it, but not today.

And then my parents died in a car accident. And how's this for irony? The fucker who hit them head on while they were coming back from a trip to Big Sur, was stoned out of his mind on drugs.

It was then I realized my dad would never see me turn my life around. My parents had given me everything—a good private school education, a stable home environment, and not only that, they believed in me. Even when I was at my lowest, stealing money from them to keep my habit afloat, my dad never threw me out on the street where I belonged. And I'd let him down.

It showed me that I was mortal. That I didn't have all the time I thought I had.

After that, I'd gotten myself clean in a hurry.

Once I kicked the drug habit, I started working fast food. I could've gotten me a car to get back and forth to the In-N-Out Burger in North Aveline Bay, but I never forgot that guy on the motorcycle. So I saved up and bought my first Harley.

One of the guys at the restaurant suggested I join Hell's Fury. I'd seen them around, coming in for burgers sometimes, so I decided to go for it.

Six months later, I wanted out.

Not only did they do stupid shit, like hazing their prospects and treating them subhuman, they weren't the nicest of guys. Blaze was the president at the time and had been a real asshole. He'd go batshit crazy over the stupidest things and have temper tantrums where all the furniture in the clubhouse would end up broken. The prospects were always charged with cleaning up his messes. I couldn't say the other guys were much better.

When I said I didn't want to be a prospect anymore, Blaze came up to me, grabbed me with his big fat fist, and told me it'd feel like I'd been fucked by a lawnmower if I left.

But I did.

I told him to go fuck himself, and when he wouldn't let me go, I laid him out flat on their clubhouse floor with a punch to the side of his head.

It didn't end there. Oh no, that was only the beginning. No one so much as looked at Blaze in a bad way if they wanted to live.

Blaze sent Fury guys after me, to do what he couldn't. Three of them broke into my house and tried to fuck me up.

I sent them back to the Fury clubhouse, all bloodied up, with their tails between their legs.

Now and then, they still tried to get to me. I'd been too quick and too powerful for them, so far.

I found my home when I met the Cobras, a few weeks after I'd left the Fury. I'd gone to the Lucky Leaf to get my bike looked at, met Drake and Hart, and they asked me about my kutte. I'd torn off the Hell's Fury prospect patch, but the outline of it was still visible. I told them that the Fury were a bunch of assholes.

We all laughed about that, and the rest was history. I joined with them a little later, quit the fast-food business and started working at the Leaf.

Now, instead of targeting me, the Fury targeted the whole club. The thought of my brothers, suffering on my account, didn't sit well with me.

I needed a drink.

Many drinks.

I didn't think I had any beer left in my fridge, so I decided to stop at the bar. The Wall was the Cobras' favorite hangout, right there on the main drag. It had shitty beer, shitty lighting, and well, smelled like shit. The one good thing about it? It was a Fury-free zone.

I wasn't in the mood for company or anything. I just wanted to grab a few beers, get home and watch the game on TV until I got shitfaced, and go to sleep.

I pulled into a space at the front of The Wall and went inside. The dive bar was packed, as it usually was on a Friday night. I waved at the bartender. A few of the regulars called out my name, and I gave them fist bumps.

"You in to play a little pool?" one of them, Gritty, an overweight, bald-as-a-cue-ball guy who helped at the Lucky Leaf on weekends, asked me.

I shook my head. "Nah. Just stopped in for a second. I'm headed home."

I was pretty resolute in that thinking. As I said those words, my eyes swept over the place, expecting to see the same old people. The same women I'd fucked, the same assholes carrying on the same conversations I had no interest in participating in.

And then my gaze landed on her.

She was facing away from me, so I hadn't even seen her best side yet. But what I saw from behind already had me interested. She had dark hair, down to the thinnest waist I'd ever seen. Wearing a little sweater so thin I could see the outline of her bra straps and a tight skirt that framed her perfect, heart-shaped ass.

I had to have been gawking, because Gritty laughed at me. "Don't bother, man. She's turned down every motherfucker in the place."

I watched her tuck a loose hair behind her ear, then grab a shot glass of clear liquid, tilt her head back, and put the glass back on the bar.

"You ever see her here?"

Gritty chuckled. "Catherine the Great? Hell no. I'd remember her."

I didn't know what he meant by that.

Didn't matter. I raked a hand through my grown out faux hawk and ran my tongue over my teeth, preparing to go in for the kill.

Gritty scoffed. "You gonna try? You feeling suicidal tonight?"

I shrugged, then tilted my neck side to side, to crack the bones there and loosen myself up. "Figure she needs a proper Zain Miller welcome."

He laughed at me. It was true. Very few hot chicks escaped The Wall without being introduced to me. But a lot of them also *left* with me, too. So I wasn't too concerned.

I sidled up beside her, between two stools, watching her. Her profile was gorgeous—her skin almost porcelain white, contrasting against her dark brown eyes. Because it was so crowded, she was pushed up tight against the bar with her tits resting on it. I couldn't stop looking at them. In the sheer sweater, I could practically see the outline of her nipples and her lace bra.

Fuck, she was the most beautiful woman I'd ever seen.

She didn't turn to acknowledge me.

Leaning my elbow on the bar, I said, "Your next one is on me pretty lady."

She stared straight ahead and said, "I am very capable of affording my own drinks, thank you very much."

Wow. I blinked. Hadn't expected that. Her accent was thick. Russian, probably. And it turned me on like nothing else.

At that moment, I had one thing on my mind, and one thing only.

Fuck going home and drinking myself silly all by myself. I had a new purpose. I wanted to leave with her.

EVIE MONROE

Chapter Four

Sasha

I walked into the crowded bar. It was definitely not fancy by any means. Crowded and full of ugly, old furnishings. What was I doing here? The finish peeled off the dark paneled walls and the low ceiling was dotted with water spots. An old jukebox spit out country music. When the door slammed, everyone—mostly beer-bellied men with too much hair and older women in too-tight mini-skirts, hair crispy with hairspray, stared at me.

Even though it was dank and hot in there and nothing like the places I used to frequent in the Red Square area of Moscow, I felt a thrill of excitement course through me. It felt like freedom.

That was something I loved about my single life.

When I was single, growing up outside of Moscow, my friends and I were poor. Our parents had barely enough to feed and clothe us. So my girlfriends and I would go to bars every night. There was not a lot of opportunity for women in Russia, so after working at GUM, the department store in Red Square, we'd all go out, trying to meet eligible men at a bar that catered to rich, foreign businessmen. We'd get them to buy us drinks and treat us, since we didn't have the money to treat ourselves.

Yes, we all dreamed of nabbing one of them and escaping the slums we lived in.

That was where I'd met Viktor.

He cruised in there, looking dashing and wealthy in a three-piece suit. The picture of success. We all stared when we saw him.

He was what all the girls called a catch, because he was both born in Russia and also a citizen of the United States, having immigrated as a teenager. So not only did we understand each other, but he gave me the thing my friends and I wanted . . . the opportunity to move to America and become an American citizen.

I wasn't very sure what he did for a living, only that he was successful, showing-off his expensive suits and watches. Some of my friends rumored he might've been involved in the Russian Bratva, but I didn't care. He never flashed a weapon or made a deal or did anything remotely shady around me. All the women swooned when he came near us. He was strong and commanding and definitely drew attention to himself.

But he'd zeroed in on me. My internal temperature went up about a thousand degrees when he leaned in to talk to me, smelling like expensive French cologne.

The first thing he said when he met me, was, "I can't take my eyes off you. You're the most beautiful woman I've ever seen."

He bought me a drink, then two. Needless to say, I fell for his charm—and him.

He said he was only in town for the summer. We'd danced a few dances that night, and then we began a courtship. He was staying at a hotel near the Kremlin, and often he'd come to visit me at GUM, bringing me expensive gifts, like diamond jewelry unlike anything I'd ever owned. I was living with my parents in a small flat outside of the city, and he was always respectful. He'd bring my mother flowers or chocolates whenever he stopped by. My mother adored him and bragged to all of her friends in the slums where we lived that I had a wealthy American suitor.

When he left to return to America, I'd gone to the airport to see him off, and he kissed me, my first real kiss. Yes, I was twenty-two and had never been kissed before. But I was from a traditional family, and that was how it was.

A lot of my friends would fly to meet their businessmen after they returned to their home country. They'd fly on the rich guy's plane ticket until they got the proper paperwork together to have them move in with them on a permanent basis. Or so they said.

My parents insisted that I not go to visit Viktor unless he offered marriage, because they warned me that many a woman had wound up trapped in a far-off country.

I didn't believe Viktor would do such a thing. I told that to Viktor, who wrote to me almost every week for a year. In every letter he told me how much he missed me. Then he called and proposed to me over the phone.

I got my Visa and flew to the United States. He met me at the airport and got married ninety days later, which was when I lost my virginity.

It was like a whirlwind romance, a fairy tale, and I truly believed I'd found my happily ever after.

But the fairy tale slowly fell apart. A few years later, I became the person my parents had warned me not to become.

Things were great for the first year. I was scared, and not speaking the language, I relied on him for everything. And he provided. I spent most of my time in the condo, not going out even to pick up the mail.

The neighbors must've thought I was being held there against my will.

But eventually, I told him that if I was going to live in America, I couldn't stay hidden away at home. I started taking ESL classes online to gain confidence. I'd always been interested in the law, so I decided to go to school for my paralegal certificate. I thought I wasn't good enough to pass Law school, so paralegal it was.

He approved of my plans but in a begrudging way. He'd say, "I don't understand why you need to work when I provide you everything you could want," or, "You know you're not smart enough in America. You're just wasting your time. Stay with me and I will take care of you." He never abused me physically. The wounds he caused were deeper inside me.

Gradually, he'd torn away at my confidence, and made me feel worthless.

Other than the schooling, he always kept tabs on me. He gave me a phone, but that didn't give me any independence. He knew the passcode for it and he could track it using his own phone, so he always knew where I was. I was not to have contacts other than him. I was to go to school and come right back. He gave me a small allowance, but if I wanted anything bigger than a pack of gum or some mints, I needed to ask him. He controlled how I spent the money, how I decorated the house, what I wore, who I saw, and what I did.

I thought things might get better when I got pregnant with Alena, but they only got worse. He controlled what I ate and made sure I exercised and constantly monitored my activity. By the time Alena was born, things got even worse. He insisted I quit the classes I was taking and devote all my time to our new baby.

So when Alena was three, I was getting in the car, it finally hit me. Did I want Alena to have a mother who was afraid of her own shadow and could barely leave the house? Or did I want her to see me as a strong, independent woman?

I left the next day. Went to a women's shelter I'd found in the yellow pages. It wasn't the nicest place, but there, I finally could let out the breath I'd been holding onto for so long.

Viktor tracked me down. Begged me to come home.

I told him no. I told him that if he continued to harass me, I'd take Alena back to Russia, and he'd never see her again. He flew into a rage, berating me in front of all the other people at the shelter. The supervisor had to call the police to take him away.

I filed a restraining order immediately, and divorce papers the next week.

Still, he came around, again and again, telling me how much he loved me, until I had to take him to court to ensure he followed the order. When they threatened to take custody of Alena away from him completely, he finally laid off. With my paralegal certificate, I knew how the legal system worked. I knew what he could and couldn't do. For the first time, I felt powerful.

Things eventually got better and in time became more civil to one another. We had reached a point where we could arrange a visitation schedule. During those visits, he'd always corner me, sometimes saying sweet things to me, sometimes giving me a guilt trip, always wanting me back. I almost caved about a thousand times.

Because yes, I knew having both a loving mom and dad was best for Alena. And yes, I still had feelings for Viktor. But not love. No, it wasn't love at all. I felt loathing.

I couldn't do it anymore. We were completely incompatible with one another. He wanted a little doll he could mold to his wishes, and I wanted to go my own way and be my own person. I didn't want to be told what to do.

He hasn't changed, I told myself as I sat at the bar and ordered another double vodka. *He's the same person I left. I have to stay strong. Move on.*

Easier said than done. It was amazing to be independent and able to take care of Alena on my own. But I was twenty-eight now. I wanted to find love, someone who would love us both and complete our family. And I hadn't been with a man in over two years.

I was lonely.

I sat at the stool at the end of the bar as a surly looking man bumped my shoulder. "Sorry, darlin'," he said with a big smile.

I looked over at him and waved him away. Typical American asshole, all bravado and machismo. He was small and weak looking, with a too-tight t-shirt. Not my type at all.

"I'm waiting for someone," I mumbled, waiving him off.

"You foreign?" he said, eyes widening with excitement, as if he'd just struck gold.

"Wow. You must be a rocket scientist."

"Aw, come on, baby. Let me buy you a drink," he said, leaning in so I could smell the whiskey on his breath.

"If you are looking to be kneed in the crotch, you've come to the right place," I mumbled to him, motioning to the bartender for another drink.

Not listening to me, he started to put down his money. I took it, ripped it in half, lifted the front of his shirt, and shoved it down there.

"I said to leave me alone. You understand?"

The man lifted the hem of his shirt out of his too-tight jeans and released the pieces of his twenty. He picked them up before they could flutter to the ground and scowled at me. "You're a crazy fucking bitch, you know that?"

I nodded, not hurt in the least. "That's nothing. Leave me alone before I show you how crazy I can be."

After that, there were a few more who tried their luck. All of them bothered me. I was lonely, but not desperate. I wanted a man who wasn't lacking in confidence. And every single one of the men reminded me of Viktor—meaning they intimidated women, probably to hide a small penis. They disgusted me.

I wondered if that meant I'd never be attracted to another man again. Maybe my experience with Viktor had ruined me, and I'd never meet one that excited me like he had.

Sighing, I ordered my third vodka double, downing it the second the bartender placed it in front of me. I'd had quite a tolerance for vodka back in Russia, but that had been a long time ago. I didn't do that kind of drinking anymore. Now, my vision swam a little.

I spun around on the barstool to see if all the men in the bar were losers like the first one who'd approached me. That was when the door opened and I saw him.

He walked inside, confidently, like he owned the place. He waved at the bartender and a couple of other people, but his eyes never landed on me. My eyes widened. He wore a leather vest and his bulging muscles strained across his tight t-shirt, and tattoos covered his arm. Dark hair, longer on top, cropped on the sides sent a message across the room: Don't fuck with me.

I smiled at that thought. He was all man. I studied his short beard and decided he had an angry, scowling look on his face. Had someone done him wrong?

He was, without a doubt, the most beautiful man I'd ever seen.

And he had confidence, too. He walked in like he was someone special, and the entire room reacted to him. Tilted toward him like flowers in the sun. He ignored it all, as if he was better than everyone else in the room.

Someone like him would probably be sure of himself. He wouldn't have to belittle a woman to make himself feel better.

I whirled back around, facing the bar, and pressed my thighs together, thinking to myself, *Dear God, if he comes and talks to me, what would I say?*

Then I ordered another vodka. I had a very good feeling I was going to need it, if I was ever going to get up the courage to flirt with this God among men.

Could I do that? I hadn't talked casually to any man since Viktor, and that was going on six years.

I brought the drink up to my lips, letting the taste settle on my tongue a little before tossing it back. With any luck, that would help calm my nerves. Maybe I'd have the courage to give him a few sultry looks.

The second I downed my drink, feeling the cool liquid slipping down my throat like water, I heard a low deep voice grumble, "Your next one is on me pretty lady."

Pretty lady? Oh, God. Oh, God. Oh, God. I couldn't look. But I could feel him beside me. My skin prickled with goosebumps and my body shot straight up like an arrow.

I didn't look at him. I remembered a little from my bar hopping days in Moscow: *Play hard to get. Men love the chase.* Gathering my courage, I said, "I am very capable of affording my own drinks, thank you very much." Squeezing my legs together to stop them from trembling.

He tensed a little, and I wasn't sure if it was in reaction to my accent or something else. I waited for him to leave. But he didn't.

"Didn't say you weren't." His voice was as smooth and delicious as melted chocolate. I fell in love with it at once. "I'm just being friendly."

I glanced over at him. *Friendly?*

Not him.

This man was all kinds of trouble.

And sexy.

And all those good naughty things.

Did I really think I'd never meet a man that thrilled me like Viktor used to?

This stranger, though nothing like Viktor, was quickly eclipsing him. I smiled. *Viktor who?*

He was even better looking up close. His hair was dark and thick, something I'd love to run my hands through, but his eyes were swimming pool light and endless. He had that same superior, cocky look to him, the look of a man who got what he wanted. But this time, I wasn't annoyed.

I was mesmerized. I must have been a sucker for a bad boy. And happy to give him whatever he asked for, on a silver platter.

"Friendly? Is that what you call it?"

His eyes almost sparkled. "What would you call it?"

"I think," I said carefully, spinning the shot glass on the bar, "you're trying to flirt with me?"

The corner of his mouth curved up in a smile. "Maybe." He pulled away a little and studied my legs.

I let out a shuddery breath. His flirting conjured up so many wicked thoughts, I was sure he could see the thump, thump, thump of my pulse under my skin.

He reached out and smoothed a strand of hair back. "So you want me to stop?"

"I want you to be careful. I'm not sure you could handle this," I said, batting my eyelashes at him.

He chuckled again. God, it felt good to flirt. Everything with Viktor had been so tense lately.

He put a palm flat against the bar and leaned in, and I could smell the cigarettes on his breath. Viktor smoked, and I never minded it, but on this man, it was an instant aphrodisiac. He breathed into my ear, "Try me, pretty lady."

My heart pounded in my chest. It'd been so long since I felt like this. Beautiful. Wanted. It was like a dead part of my body was suddenly springing to life.

He motioned to the bartender, and said, "Give us two of whatever she's having."

I smiled as the bartender placed two shot glasses in front of us and started to pour the Vodka. "Sure you can handle that, *gospodin*? That'll put hair on your chest."

He drew his glass closer, his eyes drifting over my breasts. My nipples puckered. "You have hair on your chest?"

I giggled. "Maybe. I suppose you'll never know." I held up my glass. "*Vashe zdorovie.*"

He easily tossed the drink back and motioned to the bartender for another. "I have no idea what that was but it sounded good. Did it mean you want to take me home?"

I smiled. "It means, *to your health.*"

"Oh, okay," he said, tapping his fingers. "It sounded so fucking sexy. I'm a sucker for foreign girls. So where are you from?"

I gave him a coy bat of my eyelashes. "Right here."

"Now you're really shittin' me. That ain't an Aveline Bay accent. Hell, that ain't even American."

"No, I am an American citizen," I said, taking the next glass in my hand. This was my fifth and I was feeling a little buzzy all over. "But I came from Russia seven years ago."

He stroked his chin. "Yeah? Why?"

My mind flashed back to Viktor, but I quickly squelched the thought. I didn't want to go into that. It would ruin my mood. I leaned into him, held out my hand, and said, "I'm Sasha."

"Sasha? Fuck, that's a sexy name." He took my hand in his big one, and I swear I felt something like lightning, passing between us. His eyes all but devoured me. "Zain."

"Zain?" I'd never heard that name before, but it was sexy, too. Just like him. "Do you come here a lot?"

"Some."

"And when you come here, what is you looking for?"

"What do you mean?"

"Are you looking for . . ." I searched my head for the right English word. "How do you say . . . *obshcheniye . . . companionship*?"

"Companionship?" He laughed. "You mean like a dog?"

I flushed. The alcohol was making my brain fuzzy. "I'm probably not thinking of the right word. Friends?"

"Ah. Friends. Well, today I came in looking for a six-pack but then I saw something I liked a lot better," he said with a grin, motioning to the bartender again. "And now I can't get her out of my head. Especially the thought of wrapping those legs around my waist."

Now my nipples were really puckering. I looked down and sure enough, they were beading, visible under the thin sweater. I crossed an arm over them.

The bartender started to pour two more. I held out my hands. "Oh! No! I can't drink anymore." I waved my hand in front of my flushed face. "That was my fifth."

"Your . . . *fifth*?" He sounded impressed. "How are you still upright?"

I touched my cheeks. They felt a little hot. "Five is nothing. I'm fine. I just need a little time."

He ordered a beer from the bartender and his eyes scanned over me, probing. "Yeah? If you say so."

"I do." I gave him a sideways glance, my eyes catching on the image of some tribal feathers all down one arm. He had another one, too, on the side of his neck, a snake-like thing.

I took his wrist in my hand and turned it over suddenly, admiring it. "You like painting pictures on your body," I observed. "It's called in Russia . . . *tatu*?"

"That's right. I do," he said, admiring them himself. "It's the same in English. Tattoos."

Right. I'd heard that word before, but never tested it out here in America because I never had a reason to. "Tattoos." I repeated, smiling, stroking the smooth skin of his forearm. "Yes. They're very pretty."

He was even prettier. Like a piece of artwork. Not just the tattoos, but the whole package. He had to know it. Didn't he look in the mirror? So undeniably good-looking, I was sure people could stare at him all day.

Like me, making a fool of myself, all but drooling over his skin, his eyes, his . . . tattoos.

"Pretty? They're supposed to be badass."

"Bad . . .ass?" I'd never said that word before. I laughed. "I guess they are badass."

"But those ain't nothing compared to my other ones. The *hidden* ones." He winked at me.

I raised an eyebrow. "True?"

From the way he nodded, I believed him.

"What about you?" he asked, his eyes raking my body.

"I might . . . or might not . . . have a tattoo." I winked back at him.

He chuckled. "So what'll it take for me to find out?"

I laughed. "You mean, to see if I'm a badass, too?"

"Oh hell. I can already tell you're pretty damn badass, girl. So what'll it take to let me find your tattoos?"

I hitched a shoulder. The vodka was going to my head now, making me feel not only fuzzy, but sexy and brazen, too. "Probably . . . not very much. Honestly."

His had slid over on top of mine. He leaned in, and I smelled the hint of cologne. The pure male smell fired up all of my senses. When he said, "Want to get out of here?" I nearly jumped from my seat.

I answered with a look toward the door.

He took his wallet from his back pocket, threw a couple of bills on the bar. Then he took my hand and led me across the room, waving at some men who were by the old jukebox.

Night had fallen, and I shivered a bit in the chill outside, but the cool air felt good on my skin. Holding tight to my hand, he walked me away from the entrance to a line of bushes.

He pulled me flush against him so fast that all the air left my lungs. And then he devoured my mouth with his, like he'd been practicing all his life. *Are all American men this good?*

I opened my mouth and his warm tongue slid inside, probing, flicking, making every part of my body come alive. I moaned. "Oh, God."

He pulled on my hair, yanking my head back to have access to my neck. He licked his way down and said, "I don't see any tattoos here, but I've got to do a more thorough check."

I breathed out a yes. Yes, I was ready for anything.

He motioned behind him. "My bike's over there. My house isn't far away."

I had a better idea. Looking around, I noticed a small, dark alley behind the bar. Taking his hand, my eyes never leaving his, I led him toward the back of the building, into the darkness.

Chapter Five

Zain

I could've taken her out back, and wrapped those legs around my waist, like I promised.

It wasn't like I hadn't fucked girls outside The Wall. The place was set back far from the road and backed up to a solid white fence. There was a little alley there, with a lot of trees, and the dumpsters blocking it from the parking lot made it pretty damn private. The generator outside made a lot of noise, too, so it didn't really matter how loud we got. It was good for a nice quickie.

But suddenly, I wanted more than just release.

She'd given me my second wind. Now, I wanted to play. And I wanted to see how far my little Russian princess would go for me.

I kissed her, pressing her against the wall as I slowly lifted her tight skirt up to her waist. She let me without a second thought.

She spread her legs, allowing me to cup her pussy. Did she really want everything I wanted? She seemed so ready. I slipped her panties aside and plunged my finger inside her. She was nice and wet. And so fucking tight.

I wanted to push it further. I lifted her sweater up, baring her bra. I bit at the nipples through the lace, making her nipples bead.

Fuck, her tits were perfect. I snapped the front bra clasp open and freed her tits, licking and sucking hungrily. She moaned and threw her head back.

I stepped back. I had to take in this sight.

Goddamn, she was gorgeous. Her skin was cool and inviting and smelling like candy, for God's sake, screaming to be tasted. It made my cock twitch in a way it never had. "No hair on this beautiful chest," I said, licking my lips. "No tattoos, either."

She shivered a little. "I'll let you in on a secret. I don't actually have any—"

"Hey. Don't tell me that. I'm having fun finding out on my own." I sank down to my knees and bit into tight abdomen, tasting her skin.

It was incredible, sweet and yet salty. The taste of pure woman, which I'd never be able to replicate, even with all the money and the finest restaurants in the world at my disposal. Add to that the way her soft, perfumed skin pebbled when my tongue flicked over her, and the soft, delighted little coo that escaped her mouth, I knew I wouldn't be satisfied with just one taste.

Her tiny panties, if I could call them that, were no protection from anything, merely a couple of little strings, certainly no obstacle for my tongue. I nibbled my way down, and she started to move her bottom closer to me, urging me to where she wanted me. I pressed my hands against her thighs, and yes, they were gorgeous thighs-- femininely shaped but sculpted so I could feel the muscles straining underneath.

I lifted one of her leg. She fell back against the wall as I hooked it over my shoulder, baring that perfect pink slit to me. Dipping my head down low, I pushed aside the tiny bit of fabric, and slid my tongue along her clit.

Her mouth slid open, and an "ah," escaped.

Goddamn, she was even sweeter here, a feast, all laid out for my taking. Already wet and trembling. I knew I wouldn't have to do much to send her over the edge.

But where was the fun in that?

I wanted to take my time with her.

I licked, slowly, thoroughly. Circled her clit, then lapped into it. Her noises came faster and she started to convulse, rocking her tight little body onto me. Fuck yeah. She was close.

I pulled away, sitting back on my heels, beholding the most beautiful sight. Her pussy, with the natural, fine brown hairs curling around her lips. Not shaven or waxed, like most of the women these days, but real, and unspeakably gorgeous. Her tits were high and yet had a perfect sway to them, with large, pale pink nipples. Predictably, she strained to lift her cunt toward me, pleading for more. Her face was contorted in desperation. "Please . . ."

My cock strained against my jeans. This sweet, sweet sight was almost too much for me to control. "What do you want me to do?"

She whimpered a little. "I don't . . ." she breathed.

"Yes, you do," I growled at her.

There were ridges of worry on her forehead now. I doubted I could hold true to that promise, as much as I wanted her, but she seemed to believe it. She whispered, very softly, "Fuck me."

"Fuck me, who?"

"Zain."

Just wanted to make sure she was listening. I'd make sure she never forgot my name, as long as she lived. I leaned forward. "I can't hear you."

"Fuck me, Zain," she said louder, but still not loud enough for my liking.

"What did you—?"

"Fuck me, Zain!" she screamed, unleashing a torrent of sexy Russian curses. "Please!"

And there it was. I smiled, satisfied. At that moment, I could have taken down my pants and fucked her there, hard, against the wall, with no regrets whatsoever. God, how I wanted to.

But something inside me wanted to give this girl more. To play around until she was begging me for something she knew only I could give her.

I needed to taste her again.

I came up close again, so she could feel my breath on her cunt. She wiggled her hips toward me in anticipation. Calmly, with much more control than I was feeling inside, I said to her, "I want you to scream, do you hear me? I don't want to sense that you're holding back, Sasha, because if I do, I'll stop."

She nodded eagerly. "Yes, I understand, Zain," she said, her voice not as tentative as it once had been. "Just please make me come."

The rules posted, this time I went with no hesitation, full gusto, diving in and lapping at her like a man possessed. She let out a moan, loud and confident, and her head fell back as if on an oiled hinge. "Oh, my God! Oh my God!"

I didn't have to ask if she liked it. I could tell from her short little breaths, from the way she tossed her head from side to side recklessly. I could've stayed there forever, just watching the way she reacted, her chest heaving, her stomach twitching. Listening to her deep moans of pleasure, building to an earth-shattering climax.

"Oh, Zain!" she screamed, lifting her head away from the wall as she ground her pussy against my face. She was no longer that sweet, innocent girl; her inhibitions flew out the proverbial window. "I'm so close."

"Come on my face, Sasha." I said into her cunt.

She nodded desperately.

A few seconds later, she screamed my name so loud and jerked violently forward, thrusting her hands in my hair. I plunged my middle finger deep into her wet cunt, tapping her g-spot with vigor while I sucked and licked her clit like I owned it.

Hell, I felt like I did own it!

I moved her leg and set her foot down. Then I pushed her worthless excuse for panties back into place. "You are delicious," I told her and smacked my lips.

She stood there, visibly trembling and breathing hard, sweat glistening between her perfect tits, looking spent.

But I was far from done with her.

My cock still pulsed out a drumbeat, wanting attention. But I wanted to take my time with that, too.

I smiled at her as I stood up wiped her juices off of my mouth. She reached for me, but I stopped her.

"Come to my place," I told her, my voice husky. "I want you in my bed."

She followed me without hesitation. I swear, it was like she was planted here, just for me to enjoy. And I sure as hell wasn't going to waste her.

EVIE MONROE

Chapter Six

Sasha

I'd never felt freer than when I'd hopped on the back of Zain's motorcycle and headed out into the night. He was worried that I'd be nervous about riding on his bike. He asked if I was a motorcycle virgin.

"Yes, I am. But I don't mind," I told him. "I've always wanted to ride one."

He hesitated before strapping his spare helmet onto me. I got the feeling he took a lot of women home on his bike, considering how hands-down gorgeous and sexy he was.

Not to mention, good with his tongue. *Crazy* good with his tongue. I never realized I could come that fast. *And* as the result of another person's work.

No, to say Viktor and I had a boring love life would be an understatement. This? Being with this hot, made-for-sex man? It felt like an adventure I couldn't wait to experience.

Maybe the women he took home were not as eager as I was, but I didn't see the point in hiding how excited I was to be near him. Forget shyness. I was all in.

I'd gone to the bar feeling starved for male attention, and now I had it in my sight.

When I lifted my skirt and slid onto the back of the bike without a second thought, his eyebrows shot up. He was just as impressed with my boldness as I was with his tongue.

I wasn't very familiar with the whole city of Aveline Bay. Other than the routes I traveled to go about my normal business—from my apartment to the office to daycare to Viktor's place. But I did know downtown Aveline Bay, because I'd gotten my paralegal certificate at the community college there.

We passed a number of old, stately homes along the main street with stone facades and slate roofs. I'd always admired them, thinking they must've been built in the old days by rich lawyers and doctors.

He surprised me when, instead of driving straight to the lower end part of town, Zain turned down one of the elegant tree-line streets.

I couldn't believe how quiet and dark this neighborhood was after the loud bar we'd just left; it almost seemed a sin for his bike to make as much noise as it did.

He pulled down the long driveway of a very large stone house and came to a stop, then stepped off the bike.

I slipped off the helmet and looked up at the place. It didn't fit him in the least. I expected at small, cramped bachelor pad of an apartment. "This is yours?"

"No, I thought we could break in and use their shit," he answered, taking my hand. His mouth quirked up in a smile. "Of course, it's mine. Come on."

He led me through the darkness, up the steps of a stone patio, to the back of the house. He fumbled with his keys before he finally opened the door.

He flipped on the lights, and I was shocked. I'd been expecting more opulence.

But I was wrong. The kitchen looked like it hadn't been remodeled since the seventies. Peeling wallpaper, dark cabinetry, linoleum tile floors. Worn, avocado-colored carpet stretched into the hallway.

I peered inside the hallway to see a massive foyer with a large oak staircase, as well as other rooms hidden by French doors. The wallpaper in the hallway was a dull green and orange floral. The place had beautiful bones, but it looked like it had been abandoned fifty years ago. "You live here all by yourself?"

"Yeah."

He dropped his keys and helmet on the small breakfast table and bridged the distance between us. Then he scooped a hand behind my neck and slammed his mouth into mine. His tongue explored my mouth greedily, and I responded in kind, pressing my breasts up against his broad chest.

If this was a lie, or if this was just the vodka, I didn't care. He felt damn good.

Everything he did only made the obsession to be with him stronger. I wondered what his cock was like. Would it feel as good as his tongue and fingers? Would he make me come like that again?

He kissed me deep, his hands in my hair, on the sides of my face. I tasted myself on him, inhaled the purely male scent of his cologne as he kissed me, his beard prickly on my skin.

When he broke the kiss, he reached behind my legs and lifted me up easily, so I had no choice but to wrap my legs around him. I buried my face in his neck, kissing and sucking on his delicious skin as I felt him climbing the stairs. They creaked underneath us, as did the door when he kicked it open.

Then suddenly, I was down on my back, in the middle of a bed.

A dim light came from the hallway. In the darkness, as he removed his vest, I could still see his eyes sparkling, sliding over my body like he was trying to decide what to do with me first. Then he pulled off his t-shirt, allowing me to gaze, open-mouthed at his strong chest.

"Come here," he said, leaning down and hooking his arms under my knees, dragging me toward the edge of the bed.

I looked up, past his deliciously broad chest, to those startling green eyes. He gazed back at me, heavy-lidded with a desire that mirrored my own. He scooped me up until he was standing, until he could hold my body against his, then in a dizzying turn, he sat down on the edge of the bed.

He placed his fingers on my cheek and ran a graceful trail along my jaw, down to my throat. My breathing became erratic, coming from my lungs in fits and starts. I was dizzy but strangely content as his finger traveled down my arm, to my skirt, lifting it up off my thighs.

"Fuck," he said in a husky voice. "You're so fucking sweet."

He flicked his tongue inside my mouth, then, bending over, buried his face between my breasts, tugging my sweater up to my chin and kissing the swell of my breasts.

He unhooked my bra and ran his tongue over my already hardened nipples. It wasn't the cool air blasting from the window. I was on fire. This was all him.

"Goddamn, I love your tits," he said, molding one in his hand and flicking his tongue over the nub.

My head fell back and the act of breathing escaped me.

He licked, lightly at first, and then fastened his mouth on the nipple, sucking, circling it with his tongue. I growled with more need. I didn't even realize that he'd pulled my skirt down until it fell on the floor. He wrapped his strong arms around me, cocooning me in his warm, perfect muscles. "Oh, Zain," I murmured, "I needed this."

Then he edged back onto the bed, sitting back so I could straddle him. His cock, hard and insistent, pressed through the V of my panties, straight to my center.

And he kissed me again. Harder. Deeper. Teeth and tongue, crashing and penetrating. The scruff on his jaw was a welcome pain, rubbing against my chin.

In the darkness, the only sounds were our kisses, wet and insistent, and our breaths, coming, hard, fast and tortured. I spread my thighs wide, and his hands snaked under my ass, caressing it, thumb lightly rubbing its way up and down my asscrack.

His pupils dilated, his eyelids heavy, he studied me for a second, before licking his lips and ground his cock against me. I could feel it hard and throbbing through his jeans.

"You're unbelievable, Sasha. I needed to bring you home with me because I want you in my bed all night."

He crushed his mouth onto me, and in a blink, he'd rolled over onto me, kissing my ear with a hot breath. He lifted me gently up by the arms until my head rested on the pillow, then he sank his mouth into my neck, vampire like, biting and tasting as he delivered nibbling kisses to the hollow of my throat. Meanwhile, his hand stroked ever-widening circles over my breasts, down my torso, over my abdomen. I arched to his touch, pushing my pussy up to him, wanting his fingers there.

He sensed my desire, so in-tune was he with what was going on in my head, and my body. "What do you want?" he said teasingly. "Put my hand where you want it."

Heaving a breath, I took his hand and guided it under my thong so that he was cupping my pussy, his fingers resting on the fine, curly hairs. He stroked it gently, not invasively, just barely, as if cautiously asking for the invitation to proceed. As if he hadn't had his tongue there only an hour before.

I sucked in a breath, knowing that once I gave him that invitation, all bets were off. I wasn't sure I could trust myself not to lose all control and do something embarrassing.

I couldn't help it. I wanted him too much. I spread my legs apart slightly, giving him all the access he needed.

He pressed his fingers deeper between my legs, stroking my cunt as he kissed me. He walked his fingers over my wet lips and brushed a knuckle over my clit, eliciting a moan from me. As soon as he did that, he inserted a finger deep inside me.

I ran my hands up his rock hard chest, realizing the incongruity of it all. I was nearly naked, and he was still wearing most of his clothes.

I reached for the buckle of his belt but I couldn't get it loose.

He let out a chuckle. "If you want me naked, all you have to do is ask," he said, lifting up onto his elbow and pulling open his jeans. He sat back, then stood up beside the bed and slipped them down.

Still wearing his boxer briefs, he climbed onto the bed next to me, over me, a devilish look in his eyes.

He feasted on my nipples again, licking them more, as my hands lay uselessly at my sides. I'd wanted to undress him, to taste him, but instead, I arched and bucked to the feeling of him. He withdrew a finger, only to press it back in a moment later. Kissing, nibbling, licking, and fucking me with his fingers. I moved in rhythm with him, unable to do anything but move like a puppet on his string.

Suddenly, he sat back. But before I could totally crumble, he slid his boxer briefs off, then crawled back onto the bed beside me.

I drew in an uneasy breath.

Time stopped.

Because he was a work of art. . . and massively huge, down below. I only had Viktor to compare him to, but holy cow. I never knew cocks could grow so huge.

He swept a lock of his brown hair aside on his forehead, clenching his jaw in a tight, smug smile of perfect male pride as he stared into my eyes.

Then he reached down and very slowly dragged a finger over my hip, hooking my panties, and pulling them down. He slipped them over my hips, down my thighs, and slowly lifted one leg, then the other, removing them in a slow mesmerizing dance. He tossed them on the pile of clothes on the floor and the intense way he was gazing at me, I didn't think I'd care about anything else, ever again.

I sat up and slid my leg across him, straddling his hips. He grabbed my waist and dragged me up near his cock. His eyes were pure fire as they swept over my face, down to my breasts.

Viktor and I had a lovemaking routine. A few minutes of foreplay followed by fifteen minutes of missionary position. This—me on top—had never happened. I never cared. Sex with Viktor was never about my pleasure, only his.

But Zain was all about pleasing me. Like he got off on seeing me satisfied.

And I wanted this man underneath me so much, I was ready for to do anything he wanted me to do. He could bend me any way he liked, fuck me any way he pleased, and I'd let him.

He reached under his head, under the pillow, and pulled out a condom packet. He looked nothing like the prepared Boy Scout, but he'd been around this block before, no doubt. Ripping it open with his teeth, he slid it on his cock one-handed.

He cupped my ass and lifted me off of him. His cock was heavy in my hand as I lifted it vertical, poising it directly under my pussy. "Slide onto me. Real slow," he instructed. "I want to feel every fucking inch of you as I'm going in."

He applied just the smallest bit of pressure, but it was really all me, pushing onto him. His tip touched my lips, and I adjusted, finding the right place to sink into. I took just his tip in, as he'd told me.

But feeling him pulsing beneath me, inside me, only made me more ravenous.

I loved this. Loved the control. Loved being on top.

My eyes held his, teasing, toying with him, as I gently slid down. My body shook with the desire to slam my pussy down onto him, but I did as I was told. Zain bit down on his lower lip, and clenched his hands on my hips, like he was fighting his own desires.

I moaned softly and shuddered as I took the last of him in.

This was it. This was what a real man felt like.

"You okay?" he asked, twisting a lock of my hair.

I nodded.

"I'm so fucking deep," he gritted out.

He groaned and sat up a little, twisting my hair and yanking my head back so he could bury his face in my neck as he pulled out. The next thing I knew, he rocked into me, tearing a gasp from my throat.

Tonguing my throat, he built up a rhythm. Hard and fast, then slow and gentle. He alternated the rhythm, fucking me so completely I couldn't stop moaning. My breasts pushed up against him and the sensation on my nipples rubbing his chest was nothing I'd ever felt before. I wrapped my arms tight around his back as he drilled mercilessly into me.

It didn't take long before I found myself on the edge of climax, with feelings spiraling out to my extremities, turning my entire body into a bundle of nerves. Every time he rocked his hips into me, and brought me down to meet him, he went faster, sometimes breaking the rhythm to switch things up and hit another sensitive spot within me that I didn't know existed.

"Yes, fuck me harder, Zain. Just like that," I demanded. He dragged his hands down so they were spanning my waist. He let out a growl as he guided me up and down, crashing us together, the headboard thumping louder and louder against the wall.

I ran my hand down his chest, touching each nipple, though I couldn't see them in the dark—only feel. His skin was damp with sweat, and I ached to taste the salty sweetness of it. I licked over the perfect contours of his body, tasting him. My teeth dug into his shoulder and he let out a yelp. It didn't matter, our bodies were head-to-toe slick with sweat, and we glided over each other like a well-oiled machine.

And then suddenly he held me tight and shuddered, his cock jerking inside me. Pressed together with him like that, I felt myself flying over the edge, soaring and releasing and spasming in deep, rolling waves.

Coming. I was coming again. Harder than last time, a thousand times harder.

He'd officially rocked my world. If I died right then from a heart attack, I'd have been happy.

He let out another growl, and let his head drop onto my shoulder. I was still coming, the waves subsiding, but my nipples were erect and every pore on my body was screaming in glory. Then I ground my greedy pussy on him one more time and milked what was left of the greatest orgasm I'd ever experienced.

That was it. The one event that had completely changed my life.

Before, I hated sex. And now? I wanted to grind on his cock again until he split me in two. I was completely, unabashedly, irrevocably in love with his cock.

Zain pulled out of me and rolled the condom off his dick, then tossed it in the wastebasket by his bed. I could barely move. All I could do was lie there, unable to believe what had just happened.

We rolled onto our elbows, facing each other, spending the next few minutes just taking each other in. "So, Sasha," he said, twirling a strand of my long hair on his finger. "Are you sleepy?"

I shook my head.

"What do you want to do?"

I didn't hesitate. "I want you to fuck me again."

His mouth twisted in amusement and he slipped a hand around my waist, drawing me closer to him. "Challenge accepted, pretty lady."

***

When I rolled over, I saw the light of day silhouetted around the blackout shades.

Morning.

I was shocked that I'd not only slept, but slept well, in Zain's arms. After all, he was a stranger. And I was usually very particular about how I slept. I needed darkness, absolute quiet, a lot of space, a cup of hot tea. Or at least, I thought I did.

Turned out, maybe all I needed was a night of really good sex.

I looked back at Zain, hardly able to believe that the night had been real. He lay flat on his back, his gorgeous chest exposed, one arm folded under his head. He was even more of a work of art in the light of day.

I gazed at his stunning profile; he looked somehow sexier with his hair all mussed and stretching out in different directions.

I inhaled sharply as I stared, and as memories of last night came back, my heart fluttered.

Oh, my God.

I blushed just thinking of it. I'd always been such a good girl, before. Raised by my parents to do everything right and not have one-night-stands. Actually, raised to only have sex with one man, the man I married. Hell, I'd waited until I was engaged to Viktor before sleeping with him.

As bad as I knew this was, why did it feel so incredibly good?

And why did I desperately want to fuck Zain again, despite feeling sore from all the many, *many* times before?

I wondered if he even did repeat engagements.

It was hard to believe he didn't. Because last night? He'd succeeded in making me feel like I was the only woman on earth.

How was it that some men had no clue how to treat women in bed, and then others were masters, like Zain?

I slipped out of the bed and scooted off to the bathroom, where I peed, then nearly gagged at my reflection in the mirror as I was washing up. He might have looked hotter in the morning, but I'd gone the other way.

I felt like whatever magic we'd had last night was souring now. I didn't want it to, but it was. I needed to leave before he woke up.

Quickly, I found my underwear, skirt, and sweater. Slipping them on, I looked at his sleeping form again.

I didn't want to let him go.

And maybe I didn't have to.

I scribbled out my number on a piece of paper I found in his night table and left it on the dresser.

The Wall was only a few blocks from downtown Aveline Bay, so I could easily walk back to my car.

As I opened the back door and crept down the steps, I sighed. If he didn't call, it was probably for the best. He was obviously a bad boy, and I didn't need to get tied up with that when I had Alena. Besides, if I ever found a steady guy, I'd never hear the end of it from Viktor.

So, it was probably better if we didn't see each other again.

Then I thought of him, kneeling over me, with that giant cock and that hot, smug look on his face, promising me pleasure, and I changed my mind.

EVIE MONROE

Maybe it wasn't better?

Chapter Seven

Zain

I woke up in bed, on my stomach, and blinked at the bright sun streaming in through the shades.

Rolling over, I reached out to touch the sweet little Russian princess I'd so thoroughly fucked last night.

I felt nothing, so I opened my eyes. I saw nothing but crumpled sheets and an empty bed.

I couldn't explain the feeling of disappointment that rippled through me at that moment. So this was what payback felt like. I'd usually leave first. Or, at least I'd tell the girl it was time to get the hell out. I didn't like not being in control.

But then again, a woman being in control? Goddamn sexy. Because so few women ever took the initiative with me.

God, I wanted her again.

I sat up, listening, wondering if she'd just gone to the bathroom. But all I heard was cars going by over on Main Street.

I shucked off the sheets and threw my legs over the side of the bed, stretching my aching muscles. Hell, she'd put me through a good workout last night. I wouldn't have minded having another one.

I stood up and walked naked to the bathroom, thinking about that tiny girl riding this big cock. And crying out for more. Damn. Why wasn't she here?

Fuck.

As I took a leak, I thought of the way she'd bounced on my cock, the way she'd been so fucking eager. I'd gotten her in every position I knew of, and she was game for them all.

She didn't argue with me at any of it. Are you kidding me? She constantly surprised me how much she'd been into it. More, faster, harder, again. I never thought I'd find a woman who would tire *me* out, but shit.

As tired as I was, I was also hungry as hell. I wouldn't have minded sitting her cute little ass on my face and going to town.

I splashed some water on my face and then went halfway down the stairs but everything looked just the way I'd left it. I listened for sounds of her moving but heard nothing.

I traipsed back to the bedroom. Sure enough, she'd taken all of her shit and left.

Thoughts of another round fizzled in my head, and I felt something unfamiliar grabbing at me. Disappointment.

Also, hunger.

Then I saw the piece of paper on top of my dresser. Her name and phone number. Sasha, with a little smiley face next to it.

Jack-fucking-pot.

Smiling, I looked around for my phone and realized I must've left it in my jeans. That girl had captivated me so much that I hadn't even thought of looking at my phone since . . . holy shit. I hadn't looked at it since I got to The Wall.

That had to be a record for me.

I found my jeans in a pile with my other clothes and yanked my phone out of the pocket. I had at least a dozen messages, all from my brothers. All forms of: *What the fuck happened to you.*

I opened up Cullen's first. Since he was the president, he was the priority. He'd called me twice, too. It was after ten in the morning, and he had a kid, so I wasn't worried about waking him up with a phone call. I decided to take the pussy route, though, and text him. *All's good. Just needed to blow off some steam.*

I went into the bathroom and took a shower. When I came out five minutes later, my cell phone display lit up with a call from Cullen. "Hey," I said as I sorted through my stuff for clean clothes.

"Zain." Cullen's voice was gruff.

I opened up my drawers and pulled out clean jeans, a t-shirt, and underwear, preparing for the tirade.

"Mind telling me what that little performance was last night?"

I let out a long breath. "Nothing. Just needed to get some air."

"All right, man. But that ain't cool. You need to answer your phone. With all the bullshit going on with the Fury, you can't just disappear like that."

I clenched my fists. Yeah, they were my brothers, and just looking out for me. But I looked out pretty fucking well for myself. I hated having people keeping tabs on me. And why the fuck did they need to know where I was all the time? "You want to know when I take a shit, too?"

"Zain." That was Cullen. All he had to do was say our name, and he got his message across. *Don't give me shit.*

"Fine. I get it."

"No, I don't think you do, man," he said, his voice hard. "In case you haven't heard, we're in the middle of a goddamn war with the Fury."

Of course I knew that. I was the one who'd fucking started it.

"And either you're with us, or you're against us. We have better things to do than to worry about whether or not we hurt your goddamn feelings, which is what we all thought when you left like a pussy before I adjourned. You catch my drift?"

"I'm sure as hell not with the Fury," I muttered, putting the phone on speaker and setting it down on my dresser as I looked around for my shit. Wallet? In my jeans still, from last night. Keys? No clue, but hopefully on the kitchen table. Hot girl? Fuck, what I wouldn't do to be with her instead of getting my ass reamed by Cullen.

"Right. You guys have a lot of bad blood. And that's why you of all people can't go MIA on us. They want Cobra blood, but to them, yours is the sweetest of all."

He was right about that. I hitched a shoulder, dropped the towel from my waist, and crossed the room, peering out the window. The morning was perfect, but I could never forget that no matter how perfect the day was, there were assholes in this town who wanted me dead. Not only dead but offed in the most painful way possible.

The Fury might have been after me, but they hadn't gotten to me yet. If I'd survived this long, I figured I was damn near invincible.

And I sure as hell didn't need the other Cobras playing mommy to me and putting themselves in danger in the process.

"I get it. But I don't need you guys to protect me. I can look out for myself," I assured him, jumping into my boxers and jeans, then pulling a t-shirt over my head.

"Sorry, Zain. But you should know by now it doesn't work that way. No man in this club is on his own. Someone fucks with you; they fuck with all of us.

That's how it works. So I don't want you disappearing on us again. Got it?"

There was no point in arguing. I went to the mirror, running a hand through the still-damp hair at the top of my head. "Yep. Clear."

"All right. See you down here for church in fifteen."

"Church?" Shit. I'd missed the message where he'd called it.

Cullen let out an annoyed groan. "Yeah. Church. Oh, right. I forgot. You'd left last night early and didn't get the message."

"I'll be there."

"Your ass better be, fucker," he growled. "And I swear if you're even a minute late, I ain't gonna be happy. You'll be pulling garbage duty for the rest of the year."

My insides felt like a lead weight. Garbage duty was the worst. Cleaning up the clubhouse after my brothers wreaked havoc on it was almost a full-time job. Cullen usually gave the job to our prospects, but sometimes he'd let one of us have it, whenever we fucked up. I'd done it for two weeks, last year. But for the whole year? Fuck no.

But not being late was easier said than done. I was perpetually at least a half hour late for just about everything. It was rare for me to have missed the end of last night's meeting. Usually, I missed most of the beginnings. It was the way I was wired. I never rushed. I liked to take my time.

I ended the call, stepped into my boots, and gave myself one last look in the mirror, running a hand through my thick hair. I picked up my phone and pocketed it in my jeans as I ran down the stairs. I'd wanted to call my Russian princess, but that would have to wait. Cullen was not a patient man.

EVIE MONROE

Chapter Eight

Sasha

I drove home early that morning, feeling giddy and almost drunk.

As I did, I found myself bopping along and banging the steering wheel to a Queen song, with the windows down and the wind blowing through my hair. When I stopped at a light, I noticed a bunch of young tween girls with their mom in the car next to me, giggling at me.

I smiled and waved at them as their car drove past me. They just rolled their eyes.

I didn't care. I peered at my reflection in the rear-view mirror. Who was this wild girl? The girl who let a guy tongue-fuck her in public. In a damn alley? Who slept with someone she barely knew and loved it? I looked relaxed, happy, and like someone had finally removed the stick that Viktor had wedged up my ass.

Oh, shit. Viktor.

And more importantly, Alena.

How could I have just forgotten her like that?

I pulled out my phone as I got to my apartment and dialed his number. Viktor answered on the first ring.

"*Solnyshka.*" He didn't sound happy.

"Hi," I said cheerfully. "How was your night last night?"

"It was fine. But I suppose you don't want to hear it from me. Let me put Alena on. She's just right here."

A moment's pause. "Mommy?"

My heart jumped. "Hi, *myshka!*" I said, smiling as I shoved my key into the door and pushed it open. "How is my little girl this morning?"

"Fine." For my marathon-talker, that sounded suspicious.

"Fine as in, good?"

She was quiet for a while. "It was okay. Daddy's housekeeper made macaroni for me but it had weird hard things in it, so I didn't want to eat it. But she made me. She's so mean."

"Oh . . ." I said, frowning. "Did you do anything fun with Daddy?"

"I watched a movie. *Frozen.*"

I raised an eyebrow. "With Daddy?"

"No. He was working in the other room."

I didn't think she'd have the power to get him to interrupt his work for a kid's movie, even with a bat of her big brown eyes. I was much more tolerant of children's games and movies than Viktor. I had to admit, though, even I was sick of *Frozen* after watching it for the five-thousandth time on repeat.

"Well, what are you doing now?"

"Watching television."

That really didn't sound good. "Doing anything fun today?"

"I don't think so."

I shook my head in frustration. If Viktor wanted Alena to warm up to him and not constantly dread going to his house, he needed to work with me. Take her places. Let her do stuff she actually enjoyed.

"All right. Well, remember, I'll be picking you up tomorrow afternoon," I said as cheerily as I could manage. "Can you put me on with Daddy again?"

"Okay." Then a few seconds later. "Here. I love you."

"I love you, baby. I miss you every second," I said to her, my heart twisting as I imagined her not having a good time. "And I—"

Viktor's growl interrupted my message. "What is it, Sasha?"

"Viktor. How do you expect her to be happy when she comes to see you if you toss her aside and pay her no attention while she's there?" I demanded.

He groaned. "I will. It's a bad time. I have meetings all weekend. And—"

"Then you shouldn't have taken her. It's a sacrifice, Viktor. You have to make time for her. There are many things I've given up in order to be a good mother to Alena, to be present in—"

"Not your job, though."

I threw myself on my couch and rolled my eyes. "Of course not. I need that, because your child support payments aren't enough."

That was another can of worms. Something told me he'd scammed the system during our divorce. He lived in the lap of luxury, and yet the court had investigated his income and ordered him to pay me less than five hundred dollars a month. It barely covered the rent in my awful little apartment. I'd been so happy to escape him and so new to the country that I didn't fight it. Now, I wished I had.

But it was too late for regrets. My stomach churned when he replied with the words I'd expected. "You wanted the divorce. If it were up to me, we'd be living together and none of that would be necessary, *Solnyshka*."

"Viktor—"

"Right. You don't want it. Because you want your freedom. So you have it now. Where were you last night?" he breathed out, his voice hard and taunting. "Were you with another man?"

"Viktor, I—"

"Did you let him fuck you? Did you spread your legs for him? That's a good example to set for you daughter when you could be—"

"Stop it, Viktor," I bit out. "We're done. We're through. And what I do is none of your business anymore. You understand?"

"It is my business. Since you're still mine."

"Viktor—"

"You may have a paper that says we're not married anymore. But in my head and in my heart, I know you will always be mine. You belong to—"

"Viktor, stop it!" I nearly screamed. "For the last time, I am not yours!"

He was quiet for a moment. When he spoke again, I thought maybe he'd gotten the reality into his head. But it was just more of the same.

"You're so worried about Alena's happiness. But, you're the one who tore her parents apart. You know what kind of damaging effect that has on a child? Do you--"

"Viktor," I repeated, dangerously close to hanging up. "I'm not going over this with you again!"

His voice was tight. "Then don't fucking lecture me about whether I'm doing enough to make Alena happy. You committed the worst betrayal of them all in the eyes of a child."

I tried not to let the weight of his words flatten me. It felt like a broken record, so I should've been used to this song and dance by now. But his accusations still stung.

"All right. Whatever."

"We're going to the zoo in L.A. tomorrow. We may get back late so I can just keep her another day and drop her off at daycare Monday morning."

I swallowed. The zoo would be nice for her. It sure beat sitting around, watching television all day. I almost felt guilty for opening the can of worms and calling him out for not paying attention to his daughter. But I'd just told her I'd pick her up tomorrow.

"Is Alena okay with that?"

"Yes. Of course."

I wasn't so sure she was. Alena made everything seem peachy for Viktor because she was too afraid of upsetting me. I'd hate to let her stay and then hear about it Monday afternoon. "I suppose."

"Alena would like to call you tonight since she won't have a chance tomorrow. Please be available."

And then he hung up.

I threw my phone down on the couch, ready to scream I was so angry. I needed a hot shower. In the bathroom, I turned on the water and stepped out of yesterday's clothes. The stream of hot water drummed on my back, and I tried to will it to relax me.

Fucking Viktor. I knew how he operated. He lived to worm his way under my skin. Why was I still letting him? Why did I give him that power?

Alena. That was why.

I ran my head under the water, lathering my wet hair with the sweet-scented shampoo. Sadly, I said goodbye to the smell of Zain on my skin. That spicy cologne he wore was enough to get my senses spiraling. As intoxicating as it was, I needed to wipe him totally from my body. From my memory. I couldn't afford to get caught.

When Viktor and I first ironed out the details of the divorce, Viktor said that he'd kill any man who ever touched me. When the lawyer got to him and told him he needed to calm down and change his rhetoric, he did. I thought the matter was settled, until the final hearing, when he pulled me aside and told me that if I brought any man into Alena's orbit, he'd rip his balls off and feed them to the man until he choked.

So there was a very good reason that I hadn't been with any men since we'd divorced.

But Zain? He was necessary. My little dose of sanity.

My little dose of mind-blowing, amazing sex.

My body pricked with goosebumps at the memory.

If word got to Viktor's ears that I'd let a guy take me to his house, he'd be furious. He'd probably call his lawyer and get him to weasel a new custody agreement. Considering how well his lawyer had done getting him out of the child support payments, there was a good chance he'd succeed.

And then I might not ever see Alena again.

I probably shouldn't have even left my number. That was a huge risk.

I soaped up my body, starting at the top and working down, thinking of the way Zain's hands had trailed up and down my body. He had thick, magic fingers. If any man could stand up to Viktor, Zain probably could. I got the feeling he could hold his own in a fight.

My knees buckled as I remembered just how sexy he was, thrusting into me. I had to lean against the shower wall for support. Who knew that sex could be like that? No wonder everyone always talked about it like it was the be-all and end-all.

My fingers went between my legs. Even though I was sore, I found myself stroking myself, trying to recapture a little of that feeling Zain had graced me with.

Yes, I was ready for more, thanks to that wicked, hot dangerous man.

I turned off the water and grabbed a towel. No. Casual sex had been fine when I was younger. But now, I had Alena to worry about, and she needed stability.

I couldn't let anything else get in the way of her safety. Even if Viktor and I agreed on nothing else, we agreed on that.

I wrapped the towel around me and went to my bedroom, where I stared at a picture on the dresser. It was of Viktor and me, holding a newborn Alena. Even there, I didn't look happy. It was like I already knew that being with him was not going to work out.

I set the picture face down and sighed as I slipped into some shorts and a t-shirt.

I only wished that in thinking of Alena's happiness, the bastard would have had a little room in his heart to think about mine.

Chapter Nine

Zain

I pulled my bike into a space between the line of five others, outside the clubhouse.

Shit. Late again.

I'd definitely hear all about it the second I opened the door.

Bracing myself, I gripped the doorknob and threw it open, then stepped inside.

"Nice of you to grace us with your presence!" Jet called to me.

I came up closer, threw my shit on the counter, and swept my eyes over all of them in turn, giving them each the finger. "I love you all, too."

"What happened to you, yesterday?" Drake asked, punching my shoulder as I sat down.

"I had a hot date with your mother."

"Cut it out," Cullen said, glaring at me.

I gave him an apologetic look—hell, I was only ten minutes late this time, not my usual half hour. So I was early, if he thought about it that way.

"Now that we're all here, we can get things started."

That was odd. Usually, when I was late, they carried out business without me. He stood up and pressed his palms flat on the table. "We're taking out the Fury once and for all."

Hart's eyes lit up. Jet pumped his fist. "Fuck yeah."

"What happened? We voted on this?" I asked, looking around at the other guys. This all looked like news to them. What the fuck was going on?

Cullen shook his head.

Drake leaned behind him and opened the fridge. He grabbed a few beers, one of which he tossed to me. "We voted against taking them out until we had more intel. Didn't make sense since we didn't have the numbers."

I flipped off the top on the side of the table and regarded our president. "Yeah. Last I heard you wanted to wait. Why the change?"

"You overruling our vote, boss?" asked Nix.

Cullen shook his head and smiled mysteriously. "Let's just say that I got a call from an associate. And the numbers have changed."

We all stared at him, waiting for more information. Hart asked the question that was on everyone's mind. "Who's this *associate* of yours?"

Without warning, the garage door at the back of the clubhouse roared open. A man in a suit stood there, wearing dark sunglasses.

I almost laughed. I never thought dicks in suits were half as cool as they thought they were. This guy was built like a brick shit house, though.

He walked closer, and as he came into view, I saw thick arms, a thick neck . . . fucking thick everything. He wasn't tall, but he was huge.

He set his briefcase down on the table, pulled off his sunglasses, and regarded us all with cold eyes. "I am Viktor."

The accent gave it away. Holy hell, it was like I was dealing with more Russian people these days than Americans.

Nix asked the question before I could. "Russian?"

Cullen nodded, a smug smile on his face. "Our Russian connections put us in contact with Viktor, here. He specializes in *problem-solving*."

"Problem solving? Seriously? How the hell did our Russian connections get involved in this?" I asked. In terms of our business, our Russian connections were good people. We boosted the cars, and they had a never-ending need for them. We supplied, and they paid, on time and well.

But why the fuck were they getting involved in our war with the Fury?

Cullen sat down and nodded at Viktor. "You see, Viktor's guys don't want us in a turf war. It's bad business. We spend all our time fighting the Fury; we don't have time to lift the cars. And if the Fury kicks us out of commission, it'll be even worse for the Russians. So he's here to end it."

"So wait . . ." Jet said, stroking his baby chin. "They sent us one guy to end the war? One?"

Cullen nodded.

He laughed. "Un-fucking-believable. That's like putting a fucking Band-Aid on cancer."

Cullen shook his head. "He specializes in things like this. And the best part?" Cullen gave us all a wicked smile. "The Fury won't see him coming. They know all of us, which makes it hard. Viktor can get in there and fuck them up before they even know what's hit them."

I studied the man as he removed his sunglasses to show dark eyes. Short clipped hair, a brow permanently narrowed in suspicion. He looked like a purebred Russian mafia, full of superiority and bravado. In his suit and tie, he clearly thought a lot of himself. I wanted to knock him down a peg.

"So, Viktor . . . what can you do? Walk on water? Jump tall buildings in a single bound?"

He glanced over at me, not even amused. Shit, had this guy ever smiled in his life?

He gritted his teeth and said in a thick Russian accent, "I think you should show a little appreciation, *mudak*. Because I'm here to clean up your mess."

I didn't know what the fuck he'd called me, but whatever it was, it didn't sound like a good thing.

I pushed back my chair hard and rose to my full height, a few inches taller than him. We stood there, inches apart, breathing hard, each daring the other one to blink first. The tension in the room spiraled out from us.

"Zain," Cullen hissed, urging me to stand down. I turned to him. From the look on his face, I knew exactly what he was thinking. Garbage duty, for the rest of the year. Shit.

Yeah, we had to make nice. Yeah, the guy was supposed to be on our side. But that didn't mean I had to like him. And fuck, I was on Jet's side with this. What the fuck did Cullen think one man could do? And why couldn't we take the motherfucking Fury out?

"We'll see what superman here thinks he can do," I said, looking away and stepping back from the tension.

My thoughts? Not much. It'd take a hell of a lot more than one big Russian superstar to end the war with the Fury for good. I knew that, and the rest of the Cobras did, too.

EVIE MONROE

Chapter Ten

Sasha

I spent the rest of the weekend masturbating.

Sad to admit for a reserved, well-mannered girl like me, but true.

I had all these grand plans in my head. I'd read one of the books I had waiting next to my bed. I'd clean the apartment. I'd gone shopping and get Alena some of her favorite foods as a surprise for when she came back.

I did some of those things but only half-heartedly.

Most of the time, I kept checking my phone. Almost like a robot. I didn't go more than thirty seconds without lifting it to see if I had a missed call from Zain. He was on my mind the entire time. Zain, and his massive, delicious, built-for-pleasure cock.

Which was why, in the midst of vacuuming or straightening the kitchen or some other mindless activity, my thoughts would stray to him, buried deep inside me, and my hand would stray under my shorts.

While I was trying to read, it was simply too easy to bring my hand between my legs and start flicking and rubbing. . . and daydreaming.

By Monday morning, after I'd come at least ten—maybe fifteen—times, I started to think I might be turning into a nympho. Even in the shower, as I was getting ready and promising myself I'd control my urges, I wound up pointing the stream of water from the shower massage on my clit and pinching my nipples while thinking about the way Zain had looked at me while he licked at my pussy.

The sad part was, I kept doing it, even though I was missing something.

Something vital.

The man.

And there was only one man on my mind right now.

Unfortunately—or fortunately—he hadn't called me. It was both a good and a bad thing. A good thing, considering Viktor. A bad thing, considering my pussy was aching for him.

After another orgasm, I stepped out of the shower, feeling satisfied—yet guilty. I toweled off and slipped into a professional blouse, skirt and heels. I coiled my hair into a bun at the nape of my neck to look sedate and serious.

Not like a total nymphomaniac. At least, I hoped.

I was a mother, for God's sake. A paralegal at a top firm. Not a porn star. I needed to get myself under control.

As I finished applying my make-up, I looked at my phone. At this hour, I wasn't expecting a call from Zain. He struck me as the sleep-all-day, party-all-night bad boy type.

But, I was expecting a call from Alena.

I hadn't spoken to her since Saturday night, and I missed her so much my heart hurt. I thought for sure she'd call before her daddy took her to the daycare.

I was hoping she would call me, so I wouldn't have to talk to Viktor. But now we were cutting it close, so I decided to bite the bullet and call. He answered, as usual, on the first ring. "*Solnyshka.*"

"Hi, Viktor. Can you put Alena on?"

"She's already at daycare," he grumbled.

Already? It was barely seven-thirty. I usually woke her up from bed at seven-thirty. If she went this early, she'd likely be tired by the time I arrived to pick her up. She was only four. It was too long a day for her.

I clicked my tongue. He had her schedule. He should've known this.

But I didn't want a fight like we'd had Saturday morning, rehashing the same things about my bad mothering skills, so I tamped down the argument brewing in my head and said lightly, "Oh, that's too bad. I'd wanted to say good morning to her."

"Well, you're too late."

No, you're too early, according to the schedule! I thought, but again, resisted. "I see. How was the zoo?"

"Fine," he muttered, making me wonder if he'd even gone with her. It was starting to be a habit. Everything with him was always just *fine*. "We had to cut it short as she wasn't feeling well."

My ears perked up. "Oh? Is she okay?"

"Yes, she's fine now. I'm sure she'll tell you all about it," he said, his words coming out in a rush. "I've got to go. I have a meeting."

Probably a stomachache. She always got them when she was with him. I think the stress of being there tangled her stomach into a little ball. I started to say "Okay!" but realized that he'd already hung up on me.

I sighed. Well, at least Alena was okay. I grabbed my purse, locked up the apartment, and ran to my car, wondering if I could ask one of the Simms brothers if I could leave a little early today, since I'd probably get in earlier than all of them if I started out now.

No, that wouldn't be a good idea. Likely, Marina had already told them how I dodged work last Friday. If I was a good employee, I'd be staying late, like the rest of them, to try to earn that promotion.

Sure enough, when I got to the office at 7:45, I was the first person there. If only those who got to the office early were as well-thought-of as those who stayed late. I flipped on all the lights and powered up my computer, noticing that Sarah had cleaned up the mess I'd left on my desk on Friday. I smiled and made a mental note to buy her lunch at the café sometime this week.

Then I sat down at my workstation and started to go through my email.

I had two hundred emails, all regarding various cases. I loved my job, but today, I felt myself dragging. I went to the coffee station and poured myself a cup, sucking it down even though it burned my tongue.

Back at my desk, I stared at the computer, willing myself to focus.

But my thoughts kept turning to Zain. I wondered, if he called me, could I meet him without Viktor finding out. After all, Viktor had no say over who I saw. And of course, I wouldn't bring Alena into it. I'd have to ensure her safety first.

After that? All bets were off. I practically salivated at the thought of being in bed with him again.

I crossed my legs tightly and told myself I was not a nymphomaniac.

It was the way Zain looked at me, I realized. Like I was worthy. Like I was sexy. Like he treasured me. Viktor had those cold steel eyes that always regarded me as an object, as something to use for his own gain. I had no other family in this country, and yes, I was lonely and sometimes those nights alone seemed to stretch on forever.

Zain made me feel like a woman, like someone to hold up on a pedestal and adore.

It didn't mean I was a nympho because I wanted to feel that again.

It meant that I—like everyone else in the world—just wanted to feel loved.

Chapter Eleven

Zain

Viktor took a seat at the table with us, and we all started firing questions at him.

"Where in Russia you from? You work with Maxim and our syndicate over there?" Nix asked.

He gave a curt nod. "Moscow."

"You here on a visa?" Hart asked.

"No. I'm a U.S. citizen."

"No shit. How long have you been in the states?" Jet asked.

"Since I was sixteen. Fifteen years."

"Fifteen? And how come we've never run into you before?" Nix again, peppering him with questions.

"I work up and down the coast. Not just here. Syndicate sends me where I'm needed."

It went on and on, the Cobras treating him like some science project and trying to find out all they could about him.

I couldn't give two shits. Our Moscow connections must've thought we were a bunch of pussies, hanging around with our thumbs up our asses. Sending one fucking guy to clean this up.

It rubbed me the wrong way.

Jet, who was just as pissed off as I was about it at first, now seemed to have warmed to the idea. He grabbed him a beer and asked what kind of heat he was packing. I watched as the guy pulled out a pistol I'd never seen before. Obviously foreign. A couple of the guys whistled.

"Fuck, that's a pretty piece," Hart said.

Viktor's expression didn't change. Hell, this guy was less emotional than a wall.

"I hope that ain't all you got," I muttered, looking at Cullen. "He does know we're probably up against fifty, sixty guys, right?"

Cullen opened his mouth, but Viktor spoke first. "Of course. You take out the key players, the rest of the club falls like dominos."

"I wouldn't be so sure on that."

He regarded me with a set jaw, his eyes cold. "I am sure."

"You are?" I looked at him, waiting for him to say more. He didn't. Talking, showing emotion . . . Russians had no use for any of this.

Well, at least, this Russian didn't.

I knew one sexy Russian who'd shown a hell of a lot of emotion last night. I sat back down in my chair. "Okay. So what's your plan then, hotshot?"

Viktor looked at Cullen. Cullen nodded. He leaned forward. "We'll take them out in their clubhouse. I have friends who know where to find them, and when. We wait until the officers are holding their meeting and launch our attack."

I stiffened. "Launch our attack? What are we, the fucking Navy Seals?" I snorted. Viktor looked at me but said nothing.

"Look, we'll talk more about the plan later. Right now, I'm going to go over some of the intel we have on the Fury with Viktor and we'll get together later this week," Cullen said.

I was the first one up and out of my seat. I knew we were a small club. A very small club, but to have someone come in here and brown nose Cullen like that really pissed me off. What the fuck were we here for?

I grabbed my helmet and fished my phone out of my pocket, thinking of Sasha. This Russian asshole had me craving my Russian princess.

"Wait, Zain," Cullen said, catching me before I went out the door.

I turned.

"Hey. Yo. What's with the attitude?" he asked me, his voice low.

"What do you mean?" I shrugged.

"You know. First last night, not waiting for the vote. Now with Viktor. You got something up your ass you're not telling any of us about?"

I shook my head. I didn't feel like reminding him that all this shit was because of me. "All's good."

He studied me, in that way he always did when he was trying to see inside us, pull something out of us. That was why he was our president. He may have been tough as nails, but in his own way, he cared.

"Yeah? Well, in that case, I'm really gonna need you to be civil with Viktor. We can't afford to turn him against us."

I knew that was coming. "Fine."

"He turns against us, he turns the whole syndicate against us, and we lose our biggest client. And we still have the Fury to deal with. So just . . . I don't care if you have to kiss his ass. Do it."

It wasn't a suggestion.

"And Zain..."

I groaned inside. I knew what was coming. "Garbage duty?"

He nodded. "Rest of the year."

"All right," I muttered, pushing open the door and storming outside.

But the last thing I saw? Viktor, sitting there, like a statue. Staring at me. But this time, he had a small, smug smile on his stone face. Not exactly a smile, more like a sadistic leer that said, *I've got you and your balls right where I want them.*

Fuck it all.

Picking up garbage after my brothers was a walk in the park compared to kowtowing to this asshole.

I jumped on my bike, feeling like shit until I realized I had a way to make it feel better.

My Russian princess.

I thought of her, sprawled out on my bed, naked and saying my name in that hot little accent of hers. My cock twitched.

ZAIN

That was just what I needed.

I pulled out my phone and punched in the call.

EVIE MONROE

Chapter Twelve

Sasha

"Oh, Sasha, I'm sorry if all of this goes right over your head," Marina said, giving me a stupid little sneer as she sipped from her I DON'T DO MORNINGS coffee mug. "We had a meeting late Friday night that you weren't able to attend, and some of us worked over the weekend to get the details of the case ironed out."

All heads in the conference room swung in my direction. Even Robert Simms, at the head of the table, regarded me with his mouth in a straight line. Then he said, "I don't care what had to be done to get this case ready. We're going to trial in three days. I need to know that it's where it's got to be."

"It is," Marina said, tapping her pen on her pad and giving me a look that said, "No thanks to you."

I shuffled uncomfortably in my chair. Then I looked over at Sarah, who was giving Marina the eye-daggers I so desperately wanted to give her. Then Sarah looked over at me, smiled, and rolled her eyes. She mouthed some words I couldn't quite make out.

I took a sip of my coffee, grimacing at the bitterness of it. Or maybe that was the bile in my throat from my brown-nosing co-worker.

When the meeting ended, I stood to leave. Robert Simms held up his hand, stopping me. "Sasha. Can I see you for a second?"

I swallowed. Here it comes . . .

"Close the door, would you?"

The room had emptied out and I pushed the door closed. Then I walked around the massive conference table and stood there, unsure as to whether I should sit down beside him. He motioned to the chair, and I slid it out and planted my backside on the very end. "I'm sorry about this weekend, but—"

He held up a hand. "You don't even know why I called you in here?"

I stopped abruptly and shook my head. "No."

He sat back, spreading his arms. He was a big man, not necessarily fat, but formidable. His face was lined from age, but I got the feeling that once, long ago, he might've been considered handsome.

"Then let me speak, first. Marina has been telling me that you're slacking. And I know some of the others have been complaining about it, too. You like this job, don't you?"

I nodded, lacing my hands together under the table. "I do, but my daughter—"

"Yes. I understand. We all have obligations. But the measure of a good employee is how well they cope with adversity. I know you have a lot on your plate. Maybe more than the others," he said. "But you really think I give a shit? I don't. I don't want to know what the fuck is going on in your private life. I don't care."

I nodded, my stomach beginning to roil.

"What I care about is getting the work done so that I don't look like a total asshole in court. You don't want me to look like an asshole, do you? Your job is to make me look good."

"I understand, sir," I murmured, feeling smaller and smaller.

"And everyone's scrambling to show me their best side for this promotion that's coming up. But not you. Why is that?"

I pulled myself up straight in my chair, trying to think of a diplomatic answer. I didn't think my real answer would sound so good. I didn't want the promotion because I knew it would mean having to work even longer hours away from Alena.

"Well, I would've—"

I stopped when he held up a hand. "I don't want excuses. I don't care. Just put your fucking nose to the grindstone, and get the shit done, or I'll find someone else for your position. Okay?"

I nodded. "Yes, sir. I will."

I rose to my feet, and when I opened the door, I noticed five sets of eyes that had been staring at the door, suddenly flash back to whatever work they'd been pretending to do. Of course, they'd heard the whole thing. The walls in the conference room were paper-thin.

When I trudged back to my desk and set my notepad and coffee down, Sarah peeked her head over the cubicle wall. "Are you okay?"

"What do you think? He just reamed me out for not being here enough."

She rolled her eyes. "What a prick. You're here enough. And you do stellar work."

I ignored her words of encouragement. "And I can't stay late tonight. I have to pick up Alena. She spent all weekend with her dad," I said, feeling even worse about the way I spent my weekend. I should've been working, and instead, all I was doing was taking care of myself. Now, I was in deep shit.

I tried to buckle down and get some work done, but as I opened up an email to begin working, I saw Marina walking past with a satisfied smile on her face.

I *needed* to work late tonight.

Alena was going to be so mad at me. She'd probably never talk to me again. I'd promised I'd get her from daycare. But what else could I do? If I didn't have a job, I might have no choice but to go back to Viktor. And I couldn't let that happen. Ever.

Quickly, I texted Viktor. *I have to work late tonight. Could you watch Alena tonight instead of Wednesday?*

A few moments later: *Fine. I'll pick her up from daycare.*

Well, at least he didn't argue about that. Probably because he felt guilty about not spending any time with her over the weekend as he'd promised. Not that he'd do any better tonight, but at least it was another chance.

Alena probably wouldn't be happy. But I'd make it up to her. Dinosaur chicken nuggets and cookies and cream ice cream on Tuesday night.

I set my phone down on my desk to focus on the task in front of me, but it started to ring. The display showed an unknown number, but from Aveline Bay. A thrill coursed through me. I usually didn't answer numbers I didn't know, but this time, I had a feeling.

I quickly jumped up and headed for some privacy down the hall as I brought the phone to my ear. "Hello?"

"Hey."

It was him. I'd only heard that voice that one night, and now its low, sexy timbre was forever ingrained in my memory. I started to ache for him.

"Hi."

"What are you up to?" he asked me.

Right now, I'm getting wet at the thought of you. "I'm at work," I said, almost making it to the door to the patio. The second I reached for the handle, I looked back and saw a couple of my co-workers glaring at me. Taking personal phone calls during work hours? Big no-no.

But I simply couldn't let this call go to voicemail.

"And what do you do?"

"I'm a paralegal at a law firm downtown," I answered, stepping outside into the bright light of the afternoon. "I'm busy so I can't talk long."

Unfortunately.

"That's all right. You want to meet up after you get off?"

My body buzzed with excitement. After I get off, he'll get me off. I opened my mouth to say yes when I remembered I'd be working late.

Shit. Shit shit shit.

"I'd like to. But I have to work late, tonight. I probably won't get out of here until after ten."

"That's not a problem. Text me your address, and when you're ready, I'll swing by."

I started to agree to that, but then it hit me. My house was full of Alena's toys. Did I really want him knowing I had a daughter this early? If I did, he'd probably run as fast as he could in the other direction.

"Actually, can I come by your place? I'll text you when I'm ready to leave here."

"All right. See you."

He hung up with no pretense, even before I could say good-bye, which should've made me feel a little bad. But I was too excited about seeing him again to care. As I went back inside, I did a mental inventory, making sure I'd shaved and worn sexy underwear . . . no, that wouldn't work. I always felt dirty after a day of work. I needed to go home and shower, first.

I'd just made that decision when I looked up and saw all of my co-workers giving me the stink-eye.

Right. Work first. Then sex.

I needed to focus.

That proved easier said than done.

Especially after I sat down at my desk, another text came in: *Picture my head between your legs, because that's where I'm going to be later.*

I gasped out all the air in my lungs. Instantly, that very image planted itself at the front of my brain: Zain's face, firmly planted between my legs. His tongue doing wild things, his eyes full of a rabid hunger.

I texted back: *You know I'm trying to work, right?*

He didn't respond right away. In the space of about five minutes, I think I checked my phone about four hundred times and got absolutely no work done.

Then: *Yeah. If you were here right now, I'd be working on you.*

Oh, God. He was not going to make this easy for me. I pressed my legs together and tried to ignore the heat pooling low in my belly.

I picked up my phone, just as Marina peeked her head in the opening of my cubicle. Of course she'd catch me looking at my phone. She frowned in disappointment. "Do you have that briefing I asked for?" she demanded.

I nodded. "Almost. I'm working on it."

"Well, maybe it'd be done already if you didn't have your phone surgically attached to your hand?" she suggested, sweetly but loudly, so that people on the other side of the building could probably hear.

I set my phone down. "I'll bring it to you when it's done."

"Good," she snapped, turning on her heel and walking away.

I groaned and turned to my computer. The briefing was almost done. I could make a few changes, print it out, and knock that off my to-do list.

But the second I opened the document, my eyes went to my phone again as it lit up with another message. *Your pussy is the most delicious thing I've ever put in my mouth.*

God, he was getting me so wet. So turned on. I had the urge to run to the bathroom and touch myself until

I came. As I was trying to think of something sexy to say in return, a voice whispered, "You're just begging to be on Marina's shit list, aren't you?"

I looked up to see Sarah, staring over the cubicle wall at me.

I covered the display of my phone with my hand, not that she could see it from that far away anyway. I whispered, "Just texting with Alena's daycare. She has a little fever."

Sarah tilted her head at me. "You okay? You look a little flushed yourself. Sure you didn't catch something, too?"

I felt my cheek. It was hot. "No. I'm fine."

Sarah sunk back down behind the cubicle wall, as my phone lit up again. *The first thing I'm going to do when I see you is run my tongue across your clit and suck it until you come.*

I nearly moaned aloud. I typed in: *And the second thing?*

That's a surprise. One thing I promise, you're going to come, again and again. In every room of this house.

Now I was pressing my legs together so tightly, I was surprised they didn't fuse together.

I didn't know how I made it through the rest of the day. I ticked things off my to-do list, including Marina's briefing, but I didn't do them nearly as fast as I should have. That was because every few seconds, I found my eyes drifting to my phone.

Zain sent me more and more messages throughout the day. Always referencing how much he was going to make me come, which made me so ravenous I could barely think straight. Though I'd wanted to work until ten, and hadn't finished my to-do list, but by nine-thirty, I was practically insane.

By then, even Marina had left, so I locked up the building and practically flew home. I quickly showered and changed into a little sundress, let my hair down loose, spritzed some perfume, and jumped into my car.

The second I pulled up to his driveway, I saw only one light on in the back of the house. His house was huge. And he'd texted *every room*. I shivered with anticipation.

Then I climbed up the crumbling stone driveway and knocked on the door.

A moment later, the door swung open. Zain filled the space, silhouetted in light from the room behind him. He wasn't wearing anything but jeans; even in the minimal light, his hard chest made my mouth water. I could barely make out his eyes, full of wicked intentions, and a devilish smirk on his face.

I half-waved. "H—"

Before I could finish my "hi," he reached over to me, pulled me inside, and pressed me up against the door with his powerful body. He didn't kiss me. He didn't say a word. He simply reached up under my dress and roughly pulled my panties down, over my hips.

Then he sank to his knees, threw the fabric of my dress aside, spread my legs with his big hands, and put his tongue up into my pussy, lapping at my clit. Then he wrapped his lips around it, like a man possessed, and sucked.

And sucked.

Just as he'd promised.

I tangled my hands in his hair and bucked forward as he lifted the lower half of my body off the ground and sat me down on his face, relentlessly licking and biting and sucking.

When his thick finger slid up my asshole, I went crazy. I screamed out my first orgasm, one so powerful I nearly lost consciousness. The feel of my virgin hole being assaulted by his finger while I came in gushes on his face was more than I had ever experienced in my whole life!

He may have been a dirty bad boy, but when it came to sex, he was a man of his word.

EVIE MONROE

ZAIN

Chapter Thirteen

Zain

She wobbled a little as I took her hand and led her to the living room couch. Good.

"How was work, baby?" I asked.

"I don't want to talk about it," she said in that sexy accent of hers, reaching for my jeans.

She was still trembling from my tongue. I liked seeing her undone like that. When she'd gotten here, she looked shy, and now she was in a trance.

She wanted my cock. And I was going to give it to her.

Everywhere.

Her mouth.

Her sweet cunt.

And hopefully, I would take her tight little ass.

She knelt on the old couch as she scrambled to unbutton my jeans and ease them down over my hips. My cock sprang out, rock hard for her. She took it in her hand and immediately took the tip into her mouth, like she'd been starving for me.

"Oh, shit," I said, wishing there was something I could hold onto as she slid up and down on my shaft, her tongue running circles around it inside her mouth. I felt the tip graze the back of her throat, but she didn't gag. She just kept going.

I wrapped her hair around my hand and applied pressure to the back of her head, milking it, fucking her mouth. God, it felt phenomenal. I'd been around this block before but never had a met a woman who was as eager to please me. A woman I wanted to fuck over and over again, and dammit, I couldn't seem to get enough.

"Come here," I said, pulling myself from her mouth and wrapping an arm around her waist. I lifted her up and turned her around so that she was on her knees, on the couch. "I want to be inside your tight pussy. I've been thinking about it all day."

She eagerly obliged, letting out quick, excited breaths, chest heaving as I took out the condom and slid it onto my wet dick. I moved up behind her, running the tip of my cock along the seam of her ass, and she moaned. "Please, Zain. Fuck my ass. I've never—"

"Hold on pretty lady. Let me get some lube." *Fuck yes!* I practically ran to the bathroom and brought back my handy dandy lube and slicked up my dick. Then I slowly lubed up her sweet little asshole, but not before I kissed it.

I positioned myself at her entrance with one hand, gripped her hip with the other, and pushed into her slowly, letting her ass muscles get used to my cock. She gasped as I pulled out a little, then slid in again, a little deeper. I gritted my teeth to keep from tearing up her ass. God damn, it felt good!

"Yes, Zain. More. It feels so fucking amazing. Faster. Give me all of your cock."

I didn't think I'd ever fucked a girl's ass harder. She was a petite girl, compared to me, and I still had the feeling she was delicate, but hell, I was wrong.

As I leaned over her and bit the shell of her ear, sweat rolled off my body, onto her back. Her skin was damp, creating a frictionless slide between our bodies.

She started swaying back, meeting my thrusts, until the room was filled with the sounds of our flesh slapping together and our moans growing louder by the second. When I reached around and started to play with her clit, she shouted out words in Russian, and I fucking lost it.

I groaned as I came, pulling her flush against me, so deep inside her. As I jerked inside of her, she ground her pussy on my hand and let out a scream and her asshole clenched my cock in a pulsating rhythm while her pussy flooded my fingers.

"Oh, my God," she cried out, finally saying words I understood.

I pulled out of her and we collapsed onto the couch, a pile of tangled, sweaty limbs. "Jesus," I breathed as she curled herself next to me. I put an arm around her and pulled her close to me, my lips grazing the top of her head. I opened my mouth to say more, but she'd fucked me speechless.

She grinned at me, sat up, slipped the straps of her little yellow dress off of her arms, peeling it down her body. Then she stood up and let it puddle at her feet. "Which room do you want next?"

I chuckled. "This is a big house. You sure you're up for the challenge?"

She gave me a look of defiance. I guessed it would be fun, finding out. I took a breath and started to peel the condom off my dick as she looked around. "Big house for just you."

"Yeah. Was my parents' house. They died in a car accident a few years ago. I was an only child so I inherited it. I was going to clean it out and sell it, get a place of my own, but never got around to it. All these rooms? I barely use any of them."

She turned serious. "I'm sorry to hear about your parents."

Nobody ever said that to me anymore. She was the real deal. I got up and stood in front of her, staring down at her hot naked body. My cock began to respond again, wanting to get back in the game. "Let me get rid of this," I said and sprinted to the bathroom to toss the condom.

As I walked back to her I asked, "So your choice. What room?"

She took my hand and led me toward the nearest room, the dining room, a room I hadn't used in about two years. The giant table had a layer of dust over it, but that didn't stop us from using it for what we needed.

Somewhere along the line, maybe about five rooms in, we ended up in bed. She started to nod off to sleep in my arms as I teased her for being a lightweight.

"We haven't made it through even half the rooms, yet," I murmured, pulling her close. She simply smiled and told me she had work tomorrow—which was already today, since by then, it was three in the morning. Tomorrow was another day.

And my cock was ready.

But the rest of me was tired as hell. I got maybe a couple of hours in, solid, dead-to-the-world hours. It was like I blinked, and suddenly the sun was streaming into my bedroom, and the smell of bacon and coffee hit me.

Looking over the fortress of rumpled sheets, I saw the indentation of her head on the pillow beside me and smiled. It was still a little damp from her sweaty hair, and it smelled like her, not of any perfume, but of this unique, Sasha-like smell that drove me wild. Getting up, I pulled on my boxer briefs, brushed my teeth, and went downstairs.

Sasha stood in my kitchen with oven mitts on, hair coiled in a bun, wearing my white t-shirt. It was huge on her, falling off her shoulder, and there were two little mountains rising where her nipples peaked. I don't think I'd ever seen a woman looking so effortlessly sexy.

"Breakfast?" she asked, taking off the oven mitts and starting to slice oranges at the center island. Meanwhile, her eyes were focused intently on the television.

I came up behind her and lifted the t-shirt, happy to find she was completely bare underneath. I squeezed her ass and my fingers found their way between her thighs. "I think my breakfast is right here."

She wriggled ticklishly, still watching the television. I groaned as I saw what it was. My 600-Pound Life.

"So, you're into this shit?"

She turned her head to me. "I love reality television. My guilty pleasure."

I shrugged and tried to get in her business again. I felt her in my pores, now, but I'd just brushed my teeth and was dying to taste her on my tongue again. Right now, that was what was important.

She swatted me away. "Not yet. Unless you want a burnt breakfast."

I grinned at her. "I want a burnt breakfast."

She smacked me, as I feigned innocence. I reached for her ass again. She nearly kneed me in the crotch.

"Eat the breakfast I made you, first," she said, swatting my hand away for the umpteenth time.

"All right, all right," I said to her, sighing. I slipped my arms around her and pressed her against my growing erection. "Just a little taste, though. And then you can finish."

Her mouth opened slightly as she contemplated that. "All right. A little."

She pulled me closer against her. I could feel the shiver of excitement under her skin, and it only made me want her more.

She wriggled around, smiling at me, her dark eyes sexily bleary. I lost count of the number of times we'd come last night, but we'd definitely gotten our exercise, all over the house. Unbelievably, I wanted her again. My cock rose up for the challenge. I felt giddy, like a teenager.

I wrapped my arms around her, not letting her go so easy. Eventually, she turned fully around and let me kiss her. The kiss deepened, and my hands roved underneath my t-shirt, baring those thighs. I dropped down to the ground, then hoisted her onto the edge of the counter with no protest from her.

She spread her legs wide as I didn't hesitate bringing my mouth to her pussy. She wriggled at first from the overpowering sensation when I first found her clit, but then she settled into it, gasping, pressing herself into my waiting mouth. I sucked on her, flicking my tongue over it as she moaned.

I didn't need breakfast. I loved this woman's taste. Not just loved it but craved it. My tongue went wild, lapping her up like a ravenous animal.

She arched her back, tangling her hands in my hair, saying my name over and over again and moaning. Sweetest sound on earth. When she came, I found myself not wanting to stop. I wanted to devour her whole, again and again.

"You're so fucking hot," I whispered into her skin, once I'd risen to my feet again, my mouth soaked with her juices. I sank my teeth into her neck, and she let out a gasp.

"I need you again," I growled, pushing aside my boxers as I held her there. She wanted it, I could tell, from the way she wrapped her legs around me. I thrust into her, and we both let out a breath. I fucked her hard, the way she liked.

We stared into each other's eyes as I moved against her, as she lifted her back off the counter, meeting my every thrust, hard. There was defiance in her eyes. She grasped my ass, pulling me harder, as if it wasn't enough.

She came for a second time that morning, breathing hard, and then whispered into my shoulder, "Fuck, the breakfast."

My thoughts exactly. Fuck the breakfast.

I grabbed her hair by the messy bun, yanking it enough to rip strands of hair free, lifting her face to me, fervently fucking her. As I came, unleashing hot pulses of come into her, she whispered, "No. The breakfast!"

Her eyes went behind me, and at that moment, the smoke alarm went off, and I realized the kitchen was filled with black smoke.

My eyes snapped to the stove, where a small fire was starting to lick its way toward the ceiling. She quickly uncoiled her legs from around my waist, and I pulled out of her, grabbing the pan and throwing it into the sink. Choking on black smoke, she came up close to it and sighed. "It was supposed to be bacon."

"Well, now it's cinders." I sliced a hand through the smoky air. "Ah, I'm good with coffee."

I wrapped an arm around her, feeling her ass under the shirt. My come leaked out between her thighs, onto my fingertips, and it suddenly hit me.

"Fuck. No condom."

She blinked. "Oh…" She looked down at herself. Her face flushed. "Uhm. . ." She fidgeted and looked at the clock on the wall. "Oh, God! I'm so late for work!"

She ran out of the room, peeling her t-shirt off. I followed her and found her in the foyer, hopping into her panties.

Her expression had done a one-eighty. Instead of being relaxed and sexy, now, worry creased her forehead. "What's the deal?"

She jogged into the living room and scooped her dress off the floor, shimmying into it. "It's a long story. But the basic idea is that they don't like me. I can't be late. And I have to go home and get changed, first. I can't show up wearing this."

She rushed over to me, giving me a quick peck on the cheek before trying to get past me. I slid a hand around her waist before she could and pulled her toward me. "When do I see you again? Tonight?"

Her eyes widened. "Oh. No. Not tonight. I have something to . . . do." Sounded like a lie to me, whatever it was. There was definitely something she was avoiding. But I didn't push it. "I'll call you. Or call me. Just . . . maybe don't text me like you did yesterday. I couldn't concentrate at all."

I winked at her. "Then I definitely will text you at work."

"Ha ha." She wrapped her arms around me and gave me a kiss. She let me trail my hands under her dress, and I massaged her ass. My cock jumped again. "I'll see you soon."

I watched her hurry away, then heard her car start up at the side of the house and listened to her pull down the driveway and speed down the quiet residential street. I grabbed my phone, hoping that last roll in the hay against the kitchen counter wouldn't come back to haunt us. The last thing I needed in my life was a kid. I wasn't exactly Mr. Rogers, and I'd seen how fatherhood had completely fucked with Cullen's life, and now Nix's... and Liv hadn't even had her baby yet.

I had one text, from Cullen: *Viktor wants to go over our operations to make sure Hell's Fury hasn't fucked up anything else. Come by when you can.*

I groaned. This Russian prick was really getting on my nerves.

I texted back: *Be there in twenty.*

Then I went upstairs, got myself a shower, changed into another pair of jeans and a t-shirt, and headed back toward the clubhouse.

When I got there, I noticed right away all the garbage around and cleaning I'd have to do. Fuck that. I'd pay someone to clean it up. Soon.

Most of the guys were already there, and it was clear things weren't as peaceful as they'd been a couple days ago. Drake looked pissed. He stood in front of Hart's laptop, shaking his head, saying, "I don't care what your contacts in Russia are saying. Our numbers aren't going down."

Viktor, wearing a replica of the same suit he'd been wearing last time, jabbed a thick finger at the screen. "The numbers don't lie, comrade."

"They aren't accurate," Drake said. As treasurer of the Cobras, he was in charge of inventory, and making sure we were lifting the right number of cars every month to keep up with demand. "Because of the uptick of fighting with the Fury, we've had to switch around our schedules. We had a slow start this month because of some shit that went down. But we'll make it up before the end of the month. Chill, man."

He was talking about the deal with Joel. We'd wasted a lot of time dealing with him, trying to get intel and make sure he was safe. Not to mention that the Fury had fucked up several of our grabs. So yeah, we were behind. But we didn't expect the numbers to stay down for long.

"The numbers for this month are shit," Viktor growled. "What the fuck have you *lokhi* been doing?"

Drake pounded the table and stood up. "Listen, man—"

Viktor got in his face, staring him down, nose to nose. "No, you listen. While you've been fucking around like *deti*, your business is getting away from you."

I put a hand on Viktor's shoulder, trying to pull him away. "Dude. It's fine. Once we end the Fury, the production will go back to normal."

He stared at my hand like it was infected. "It's not fine. Your operation has been bringing up the longest lead-time and the smallest returns of any of the West Coast operations. The syndicate does not like this. They'll find someone else to get them what they need."

We didn't doubt it. The Cobras did a damn good job, for the number of men we had. But we were a small club, and there were bigger fish out there that could probably turn over more inventory. And yeah, the Fury's shit had cut into our operations. We were running at full bore, but I wasn't going to be the person to admit that Viktor was right—our inventory was lacking more than we wanted to admit.

But this asshole was bluffing. He knew the syndicate wouldn't take our business from us. We delivered, and with a lot less of the red tape the other operations made them cut through.

"Go right ahead," I grunted, defiant. "You go ahead and see what they say."

He didn't miss a beat. He reached into his jacket pocket and pulled out his phone. "I will do that."

Then he strode out of the clubhouse, not looking back. I looked at Drake and shook my head. Drake dragged a hand down his face. "That asshole's really getting on my nerves."

Cullen, who'd been out back readying a new vehicle to ship overseas, appeared in the garage bay. "Where's Viktor?"

"Out front, playing with himself," Drake muttered.

Cullen looked at me for the answer, so I gave it. "He was complaining our take was slow this month, so he threatened to call the syndicate and report us. I told him to go ahead."

Cullen frowned. "Did you tell him the reason why? That it's the fuckin' Fury? That that's the only reason that big motherfucker's here?"

"Yeah, we told him," I grumbled, going to the fridge and getting a beer. "The fucker's an asshole. He doesn't want to listen. He just wants to create trouble. We're hanging all our hopes on this guy? Seriously?"

Next to me, Drake nodded. At least he was on my side.

Cullen glared at both of us. "Look. I hate it as much as you do. But talking to Maben in Russia, he gave me his word this Viktor fucker could take care of the Fury and none of it would come back on us. He's our only chance to get rid of the Fury and keep things going. You got that? So if he says jump, we jump. Just for a week or so. Then back to normal. You hear me?"

I looked at Drake, who scratched his temple and hitched a shoulder. "Yeah. Okay," he said, beaten.

Cullen gave me a look, waiting for me to the say the same. Fuck it. "Fine."

Cullen cupped his hand around his ear. "I didn't hear you."

"Fine," I said, louder. What did he expect, for me to go and suck his dick?

"Good." He headed for the front door. "Now I guess I have to go kiss some ass on your behalf. But next time, man, you're cleaning it up yourself, so there better not be a next time."

As he strode away, instinctively, both Drake and I gave him the double-middle-finger salute behind his back.

But Cullen always had a radar for that. He held up both of his middle fingers, back at us.

"I'm serious, guys," he called as he went to the front of the clubhouse, where Viktor had gone. "If either of you fuck this up, I'll have your heads. And Zain. . .clean this shithole up already! It's your job!"

ZAIN

Drake gave me a look that echoed everything I was thinking. We knew not to mess with Cullen, because he meant every word he said. But dammit, I'd never been so close to throwing down with him.

EVIE MONROE

Chapter Fourteen

Sasha

Somehow, I managed to get into work without being *too* late.

Only fifteen minutes.

That was a small miracle, considering I'd driven like a madwoman to my apartment, showered, changed, and driven back to the office, all in the space of twenty-five minutes.

Unfortunately, fifteen minutes was still an offense punishable by death. Or at least, one would've thought that, from the looks Marina gave me.

"Look who showed up!" she called jovially as I stepped inside. "So glad you decided to join us, Sasha."

I fought the urge to jump on her and poke her eyes out as I walked past her to my cubicle.

"I closed up last night," I reminded her gently.

"Oh. About that," she said, giving me a plastic smile. "You forgot to turn off the front lights. Mr. Simms doesn't want us wasting electricity, you know. He was furious."

Damn. Had I forgotten the lights? I'd been too excited about meeting Zain that I'd rushed out like a bullet shot from a gun. "Well, I—"

"And your shirt's unbuttoned. I can see almost all your assets," she said, leaning in as if to whisper, but still speaking so loudly that some of the men in the office turned to check us out.

I looked down. Sure enough, I'd missed a couple buttons on my blouse. I started to button them, my cheeks flushing.

"Or maybe *that's* the way you're hoping to get ahead in the office?" she asked sweetly. "I've heard that works. You're young and attractive. I suppose it wouldn't hurt your case to throw those assets around. At this point, you've been late so many times, if he did hire you for Senior Paralegal, that would be the only way to explain it."

I scowled at her as Sarah appeared, her face twisted in disgust. She must've heard the last comment. "Shut up, Marina. Geez, you can be such a bitch."

Marina blinked innocently. "What? She's trying to get ahead by using her sex appeal instead of good old-fashioned hard work, and I'm the bitch?"

"I missed a button on my blouse," I said to her, my voice rising. "That's all. It wasn't intentional."

"Riiiight," she said, drawing the word out like she didn't believe me. She turned and sauntered back to her cubicle, swinging her wide hips in her bright, hot-pink boucle suit that probably cost more than my rent for the year.

Sarah touched my shoulder and whispered, "Don't mind her. Is everything okay? Alena's all right?"

I nodded and walked to my cubicle to set my things down so Robert wouldn't see me, looking like I'd just walked in, even though I had. It didn't matter—he probably already knew I'd arrived late. Knowing Marina, she'd already sent him an email.

"You look a little. . . stressed?" Sarah said, tilting her head as she inspected me over the cubicle wall. "Is Alena still sick?"

I leaned over to switch on my computer, then felt my hair to make sure it was all still neatly twisted in the bun. "Nope. All's good. Just overslept a little."

She eyed me warily but eventually sat down to do her own work. The moment I was alone and had a second to concentrate, it hit me.

I still hadn't called Viktor to check on Alena.

That was bad of me. I'd called her last night while I was still at the office working late. I told her I'd pick her up tonight, and we'd get those chicken nuggets and ice cream. She'd been less than enthusiastic about spending another night with her dad, but I promised I'd make it up to her.

And what had I done? I'd let another day go by without calling to wish her a good morning.

Cursing myself, I quickly dialed Viktor's number. I let it ring four times before deciding he must already be working and didn't want to be disturbed. I ended the call and texted: *Sorry. Late night last night. Hope everything is ok with Alena.*

A moment later, he responded with: *Y.*

That was it. Just: *Y.*

Which told me he was pissed at me. Right. Because my having a career and working late wasn't important in his book. Also, though I knew there was no way he could have known what I'd been up to after work, I still felt a little guilty. I didn't have time for Alena, and yet I'd had time for Zain. And also, I couldn't help feeling like Viktor had found out. He'd once told me, right before I'd left him, that he had eyes everywhere.

No. If he'd found out what I'd been up to, he wouldn't just be pissed.

He'd probably be so jealous, he'd kill me. Maybe not kill me, but he'd rip me a new asshole and make me wish I were dead.

My mouth went dry at the thought.

Somehow, I managed to buckle down and work the rest of the day without incident. I worked an extra half-hour, too. Long enough to make up for arriving fifteen minutes late, but not long enough to avoid Marina's, "Oh, Sasha, are you taking a half day?" when I tried to slip out unnoticed.

But I had to get to Alena. I missed her so much, my heart hurt.

And I also felt guilty. Like I'd abandoned her and put my needs in front of hers. I tried to remind myself that wasn't the case. The court had her visiting her father on weekends, and I'd had to work late yesterday. I hadn't just skipped out because I wanted to shack up with Zain. I'd never do that.

As I drove, my route took me along the beach. The setting sun painted orange rays across a canvas of pale blue sky. I loved California. Even though I threatened Viktor with taking Alena back to Russia, I didn't think I'd ever truly go. Moscow was dreary. The California sun, the ocean, the people . . . this was my true home. I'd never been close to my family, so there wasn't anything in Moscow to go back to. I'd been such a shy, sheltered little mouse back then. In so many ways, I'd become a new woman since leaving there.

And I'd become even more different since leaving Viktor.

Now, I was independent. I was confident. I was an American woman. The kind of woman I wanted to be for Alena's sake.

I smiled as I stopped at a traffic light. My eyes trailed out the driver's side window, to a series of one-story warehouses on the wharf. Nothing very intriguing. I passed this way almost every day, and it was usually the same scene. Men in work clothes, going home from their jobs, a few seagulls, strutting around on the pavement looking for scraps, and beyond that, the placid ocean, glimmering in the sunset.

But today, something made me pause.

I blink, refocused, and looked closer.

A stocky man stood on the pier in a dark suit, his phone pressed up against his ear. He looked like a million dollars.

I'd been married to Viktor for years. I knew him when I saw him.

But I also knew the man standing beside him, too. Not as well, but just as intimately.

No one could mistake that physique. The way he filled out those jeans. The way the long part of his hair caught the breeze.

Zain.

I watched them, transfixed. In many ways, they looked like opposites—the successful, buttoned up businessman and the rough-and-tumble, laid-back working class man. Why were they together, in the same picture? It made my mind go haywire. Surely my mind was playing tricks on me, with these two different parts of my life thrust together like this.

ZAIN

I blinked and watched as Viktor brought the phone from his ear and said something to Zain. In a moment, Zain said something back.

They knew each other.

My lover and my ex-husband knew each other.

How in the world did they know each other?

I momentarily forgot how to breathe. I found myself gasping as I watched the pair of men open a door to one of the warehouses and go inside. I kept staring at that door, even after it closed. I stared, until the driver behind me beeped his horn, and I realized the traffic had moved on.

Pressing on the gas, my head swam. My heart beat madly in my chest. Maybe Viktor really did have eyes everywhere. Maybe Zain was his eyes.

Had Viktor hired Zain to spy on me?

No, that couldn't be right. I didn't put it past Viktor to hire someone to spy on me, but if Viktor found out that that person had been fucking me, too?

He wouldn't be alive. Viktor would have already killed him.

Unless Viktor didn't know.

And he couldn't know.

As I drove to the daycare to pick up Alena, my neck prickled. I felt like I was being followed.

I went inside and breathed a sigh of relief and joy as Alena rushed up to me. I wrapped her in a hug, but she didn't greet me with a smile as she usually did. Her eyes were rimmed with distrust.

"Where were you, Mommy?" she asked, pouting.

"I'm sorry, honey," I replied, inhaling the scent of her sweet shampoo. "I got caught up at work. Chicken nuggets and ice cream?"

She contemplated this. "Cookies and cream?"

"Of course."

Her face brightened. Instantly, she forgave me.

I tried to savor that moment, the exquisite perfectness of being with the little girl I adored, my baby, but something still tugged at my nerves.

Whatever reason Zain and Viktor had for being together, it wasn't good. It couldn't have been. I couldn't trust either of them.

And whatever Zain and I had? It couldn't continue.

It ended now.

EVIE MONROE

Chapter Fifteen

Zain

After doing a little song-and-dance and kissing a little more Russian ass, we finally got Viktor to calm down.

It wasn't easy.

When I went outside with a plastic bag of garbage and tossed it in the dumpster, Viktor was on the phone with the syndicate, talking a mile a minute in Russian, while Cullen tried to get a word in edgewise. Eventually, Viktor hung up and started listening to Cullen. As usual, diplomatic Cullen was able to talk him off the ledge and get him to continue backing us.

I backed Cullen up, playing nice, even though what I really wanted to do was throw down with the Russian asshole who thought his shit didn't stink.

Then, I went back home. Took a shower. Realized it was too late to text Sasha at work and throw off her concentration, since she was probably at home by then. Didn't care. Thought of her squirming a little when I typed in: *I want you under me right now.*

I stared at the screen, expecting a response right away. Didn't get one.

I wasn't too worried. It was nearly dinnertime, so she wasn't chained to her desk at work.

When I looked again, she still hadn't responded. Not only that, it said the message had been read.

All right. She was ignoring me. That was when I started to think something was wrong.

It wasn't normal for women to ignore me. It wasn't ego speaking, that was just my reality. Women came when I called. They didn't turn down my invitations. Hell, I usually didn't even have to invite them. They came after me.

And I sure as hell never had to wait when I sent a hot text to a woman.

I told myself it didn't fucking matter. I had plenty of other women out there that I could fuck.

I didn't like surrendering control to this woman, but hell. It made me want her all the more. Her, and only her.

As I made myself dinner and sat down to watch the ball game, I drank a beer and tried to convince myself I wasn't horny as hell.

When that didn't work, I tried to convince myself that any woman would help satisfy the need.

That didn't work, either. I dreaded calling any of my usual women. They wouldn't fill the need inside me. Only Sasha could do that.

And that was fucked up.

I'd told myself long ago, I would never let a woman matter to me like that. I had women out the ears, and I liked that about my life. I liked having my choice, never getting too serious about any of them. This huge house of mine wasn't a bachelor pad, but that sure as hell didn't mean I wanted a girl coming in and making it look all *special*. I loved living alone.

What I really needed to do? Fuck her again. Fuck her once more, and maybe that'd get her out of my system.

Deciding on my new plan of attack, my blood started pumping. I picked up my phone, and this time, I called her.

No answer.

Fuck it all.

I clenched my hand into a fist so hard that it shook. Then, I called again. This time, it went right to voicemail.

What. The. Fuck.

Was she ignoring me?

Nobody fucking did that to me. Nobody.

Fine. If she was going to ignore me, then I'd do it right back to her. Delete her number. Forget about her. Done.

ZAIN

I hovered my finger over the *delete contact* button for about thirty seconds. Then I decided that maybe I was being too quick with my trigger finger.

Maybe she was just in the shower, or busy.

I'd call her again tomorrow.

If she didn't answer, then I'd delete her.

***

The following morning, when she didn't answer, I nearly threw my phone against a wall. But that was it. No more calls. I'd be fucked if I let some hot Russian chick do that to me. Who the fuck did she think she was? She wasn't that gorgeous. She had a little space between her two front teeth. She had nice tits, but she was a little soft, no definition in her muscles . . .

I shoved those thoughts away when I realized I was getting hard, just thinking of her.

No use denying it to make myself feel better. My Russian princess was hot as fuck and. . . clearly not mine anymore.

This kind of torture went on for a full week. I'd call, she wouldn't answer. I'd flirt with deleting her number, but never could. I'd send her a text, she wouldn't respond. I'd hurl curses into the air, tell myself I should go to The Wall, grab any girl, and fuck her brains out, to numb the self-destructive feelings biting at me. Then I'd only feel worse, because I knew it wouldn't work.

Suddenly I felt a little guilty for treating all the women in my life that way. Because getting this little dose of my own medicine was a pain worse than death.

Finally, I decided that if I endured much more of this, I'd go batshit crazy.

Viktor was giving us shit and kowtowing to him and doing his bidding was really starting to get old. So not only was Viktor fucking me, I felt like Sasha was fucking me, too. So basically, I was being fucked in every hole by the Russians, and still as horny as ever.

I knew I had to do something about it.

So, as soon as I pulled into the parking lot for the clubhouse, I punched in a call. One last time, I told myself.

It didn't go through.

I frowned and typed in a text to her, wondering what that meant. A little red exclamation point showed up next to it, saying it could not be delivered.

Wait . . . had she blocked my number?

Oh, fuck no. I couldn't let her get away with that. I stormed into the clubhouse on a tear. The guys said hey to me, but I ignored them, staring at my phone like I was trying to decode all the mysteries of the universe.

While we all sat there at the clubhouse watching Viktor go over the latest inventory with Drake, I Googled, *Sasha Aveline Bay.*

I got a huge number of search results. Fuck. Why hadn't I found out her last name? Why had I not insisted I meet her at her place? This would be impossible.

Then I remembered what she said she did for a living.

I typed in: *Sasha paralegal Aveline Bay*

Suddenly, her picture popped up, as part of a website for Simms & Simms, attorneys at law. They had offices at the business complex right down the street.

I smiled and closed my hand into a fist, pumping it under the table in silent victory. Shifting in my seat, I took note of her last name: Kotov.

I typed into the search bar: *Sasha Kotov, Aveline Bay.*

Several search results popped up, the first ones for those criminal background check services that allow a person to research another person for a fee. But I didn't need to do that. One of the websites gave her whole address. Cavendish Village, 1201 Monterey Lane, Apartment 2B.

Jack-motherfucking-pot.

The second the meeting ended, I jumped up and said goodbye. I had somewhere to be.

ZAIN

She could ignore me all she wanted, via the phone. But no way in hell could any woman ignore Zain Miller in person.

At least, I sure fucking hoped so. I'd gone insane enough as it was.

EVIE MONROE

Chapter Sixteen

Sasha

I was beyond happy the following Monday after I picked up Alena from daycare.

Happy, but not exactly satisfied.

Seeing her face always filled me with joy. She was the light of my life. But having a light in one's life didn't eliminate the need for the dark.

The dark in the form of my delicious badass. The lying, scum-sucking, but yes—still delicious—badass that I'd had to force out of my thoughts.

Zain had called me a few times and texted me, too. But I'd made the decision that I couldn't trust him. And as much as I wanted to be with him, as much as my every pore seemed to scream for the way he'd made me feel . . . I couldn't. So I deleted his number. And then, when he called me again, I blocked him.

Done.

Gone.

But not forgotten.

Oh, definitely not forgotten.

Luckily, though, Viktor hadn't mentioned anything about Zain to me when I'd dropped Alena off for her weekend visit. I'd gone there, bracing myself for the onslaught, but it never came. And because Zain had still called me up until a few days ago, I knew Viktor hadn't killed him yet. So my hope was that if I waited long enough, everything would blow over, and I'd be in the clear.

Well, not fully in the clear.

Because even though I'd deleted Zain's number and done my best to force him out of my head, I was still crazy for him. Work sucked. Being a single mother sucked. Dealing with Viktor sucked. It was all so stressful. And he was my sweet release.

Now, I felt like a volcano, ready to blow its top.

I thought that it was only a matter of time before I showed up at his house, begging for him to take me, one last time. However he wanted. Viktor be damned.

"Mommy, look at this!" Alena called for the thousandth time from the living room as I stood in front of the stovetop, stirring the macaroni for the Kraft dinner we were about to have.

"That's nice, honey!" I called, throwing the chicken nuggets into the oven as I mentally searched the freezer for a vegetable that would go with tonight's gourmet dinner.

"Mommy! Mommy! Mommy!"

It was always this way, whenever I got Alena back from her weekend trips to her father's. Alena came home from her daddy's starved for attention because at Viktor's, everyone ignored her. She knew how easily she could get my attention when I hadn't seen her in a few days. And she milked it, constantly wanting to show me everything she did. I loved this time. I wanted to plaster myself to her side and never let her go, but I also had to get her dinner, give her a bath, read her a story, and tuck her into bed at a decent hour. None of these things would get done unless I hustled.

"That's nice!" I called again, reaching into the freezer for some carrot medallions and noticing that I'd finished off the cookies and cream ice cream. I'd hear about that from her later.

I threw the carrots into a dish and filled it with water, then shoved it in the microwave. My mind stayed on Alena, thinking that I should probably sign her up for some ballet lessons at the school right near the daycare. They offered a class for four-year-olds on Tuesdays. Viktor and I had always agreed ballet would be a good activity for her. He'd told me that he'd pay the tuition, too, which was a plus.

"Mommy! Look at me!" Alena called from the doorway.

I whirled to set the table, grabbing the dishes and napkins off the counter when I caught sight of Alena, standing there. "That's nice, ho—"

I stopped, dead. As did my heart.

"Mommy! I was murdered!"

I shrieked.

For a split second, I thought she really was. I thought she was covered— head-to-toe—in blood.

But her smile was bright white among all the red, and there was just too much blood for anyone to come out smiling.

Suddenly I remembered the acrylic paint her father had bought her for her fourth birthday, complete with an easel that didn't fit so well in my tiny apartment. Alena had been thrilled; I'd been cautious. For this very reason.

"What did you do?" I cried, ready to break down in tears. I braced myself as I went to the doorway and peered into the living room.

It was worse than I expected. It looked like a murder scene, if the killer had chopped the person up into tiny pieces and smeared the blood all over the walls.

I fell to my knees, all the while fighting the urge to bawl. I couldn't let Alena see me like that. Not after I'd worked so hard to be a strong role model for her.

I blinked back the tears. "Alena!" I said in my sternest voice. "What did I tell you about those paints?"

She started to pout.

I surveyed the damage and realized she'd gotten paint all over the sofa, the coffee table, the television—every piece of furniture in the damn room was covered in red. "I told you that they were for the paper! Not for painting yourself!"

"But I was murdered!" she repeated, as if trying to convince me.

I tilted my head. What four-year-old knew about murder? "Was daddy letting you watch some of his movies?"

Viktor loved those stupid gangster movies with high body counts and lots of gore. That was all he used to watch when we were together.

She gave me a wide-eyed, innocent look. "Yes! We watched TV!"

I gritted my teeth and made a mental note to have it out with him next time I talked to him. We'd gotten along well the last time I dropped Alena off, but if he kept doing pea-brained things like this, things that were against my explicit wishes, we'd have to have a talk.

Obviously, he didn't care. We'd had this argument before.

Maybe I shouldn't bring it up, I thought as I began cleaning up the mess. Maybe he'd done that for a reason. Maybe he was waiting for me to do something wrong with Alena, so he could bring up Zain and add fuel to the fire. And what a fire that would be. Talk about explosive.

I decided that I should just let it lie. Wait until things blew over.

Sighing, I went down the hall to start up the bath. As I turned the faucet for the tub and put the stopper in the drain, the doorbell rang.

Perfect.

Switching directions, I went to answer it, noticing that Alena was now writing her name—or at least, trying to write her name, she got the N backwards—on the wall in red paint. "Stop that!" I shouted, picking her up and holding her on my hip. Paint now splattered across the front of my blouse.

"You're a little beast, you know that? A cute—but lethal—little beast!"

In response, she took her paint-covered finger and drew a red line on my face. I pushed her hand away, then swooped down and yanked open the door.

And I might have died right there.

Standing in front of me, looking as stunned as a big, strong badass, was Zain.

Chapter Seventeen

Zain

Well, fuck me.

The whole sight in front of me was one big mindfuck. Sasha, standing in the doorway of her apartment over this shitty Chinese restaurant in the worst section of town, with a curly-haired little tot on her hip, covered in what looked like blood.

Inhaling, I smelled the stench of paint, mingling with the scent of Chinese food, wafting up from downstairs. So that explained away why they were covered in red.

But it didn't explain the kid. "This little one yours?" I asked, reaching over to touch her hand.

The little girl took one look at me and started to scream bloody murder.

Sasha put her down and the girl ran off into the apartment, still screaming. "Yes. Her name is Alena."

I could've said something about how I didn't know she had a kid, but as I watched her looking helplessly down at the puddles of red all over the place, I realized I didn't know *Sasha* that well, either.

She was a mom.

Now, looking at her, at the warmth in her eyes, at the way she looked at the kid like it was her favorite thing on earth, I saw it. Of course she was a mom.

Before I could say anything, something in the kitchen made a sizzling noise and her eyes widened. "Shit!"

She ran into the apartment, leaving me in the doorway. I took a few steps in. Either she was in the midst of a really weird redecorating project, or that little stinker had gotten the place good. There were red fingerprints on almost every surface. I moved around it carefully, trying not to get any on my boots and make it worse.

I found Sasha over the kitchen sink, throwing some noodles through a strainer. It smelled like something had been burning. "You're good at burning shit, ain't ya?"

She scowled at me in response.

"Need help?"

"I've got it!" she yelled, as I checked the stovetop. Looked like burned dinosaur nuggets and macaroni and cheese. She ran to the fridge and grabbed a tub of margarine, ignoring me.

The little girl started to scream, "Mommy! Mommy!"

Sasha rolled her eyes to the ceiling. Her lips moved, but she didn't say anything. She may have been saying a silent prayer. So she'd take God's help, but not mine? She must've really hated me.

I set my helmet down on a counter and walked down the hallway. A light was on in the bathroom. When I got there, I peered in. The little kid was inside, staring at the tub behind a rubber-ducky shower curtain, which was starting to overflow.

I reached in and twisted the knob to turn it off, then gave the little kid a smile.

She screamed even louder than before and backed up flat against the wall.

Funny. I had that kind of reputation with most kids. I'm not sure what it was that made me scare the shit out of them, but I'd been fine with it. Never really cared about them.

I held up my hands in surrender and backed away, nearly stepping on Sasha, who was storming down the hallway like a bat out of hell.

"What did you do?" she asked, suspicious.

"Nothing. I . . ." I pointed to the tub. "You almost had a big problem. I turned off the water. So sue me."

She looked at the kid, who was still letting out this scream like a fire alarm. "Alena. Zip it," she growled, looking at me. "As you can see, I'm busy at the moment."

"That's why I asked you if you needed help."

She sighed. "Yes. Mental help. But nothing you can give me right now. I have to bathe her and feed her."

"If you take care of the bath, I'll get the food on the plates," I said, heading toward the kitchen.

She paused for a moment, and then called, "Zain!"

I turned to see her peeking her head out the door. "I don't have enough for three."

"That's okay. I already ate," I lied, giving her my lady-killing smirk that I knew would make her rue the day she never texted me back. "Seriously. I don't want anything from you. I just want to help. Okay?"

It wasn't totally true—obviously, I wanted what was inside those tiny panties—but I could put that on hold for now. A touch of a smile appeared on her lips. "Okay. Thanks."

She went back into the bathroom while I headed to the kitchen. The kitchen was small and outdated, with old beige appliances, but from the homey little touches she'd put there, it was clear a woman lived here. Unlike my place, which hadn't seen a woman's touch since my mom died.

And, judging from the finger paintings proudly displayed on the fridge, it was also clear a *kid* lived here.

No wonder she hadn't wanted me anywhere near this place. Even if she only had joint custody, a kid wasn't something a person could easily hide.

I found two plates and put the food on them, then grabbed a couple of glasses. "What do you two drink?" I called.

"Oh. Milk for her, in the princess sippy cup . . . water for me, please," she called over the sound of her kid splashing and giggling in the tub.

I had it all set out for her by the time the little girl appeared, wearing a princess nightgown and wet hair. She looked a lot cuter, now that she wasn't covered in paint.

ZAIN

Sasha said, "Now Alena. I want you to eat your food, and then go to your room. I don't want you setting foot in the living room until I get it cleaned up."

"Yes, mommy," the little girl said, running to the table and climbing onto the chair. She frowned at the dinosaur nuggets. "They're black."

Sasha came to the table still wearing her blouse and skirt, her work outfit I assumed, splashed with red. Her straight hair fell in her face and her eyes were dull with fatigue. She slumped into the chair and ordered, "Just eat it and don't complain."

The kid pouted and sunk into her chair. She picked up one of the nuggets and banged it against the plate. Then she pouted and stuck out her tongue at me, the stranger. "I don't like this."

"Drink your milk and eat," Sasha said flatly, nudging the sippy cup toward her as the girl shoved an entire nugget into her mouth. She chewed slowly, disgust on her face.

Then she grabbed a napkin and spit the mouthful into it.

"Okay," she said to Alena, who was still poking the food with her fork. "Just a few mouthfuls of mac and cheese and I'll let you go."

The little girl shoved in a couple mouthfuls, and said, "Ice cream?"

Sasha shook her head. "Sorry. None left."

The little girl's brows tangled together as she considered her options. "Can I go play, please?"

Sasha nodded. "*May* I. All right. But in your room. I put your Barbies under your bed, if you're looking for them."

Alena jumped from her chair and went into the hall, still glaring at me.

When she was gone, I grinned at her. "I don't think your girl likes me very much."

She shrugged. "Can you blame her? You're about ten times her size. If I were her, I'd be scared, too." She lifted the plates and dropped them into the sink. "Don't you like kids?"

"Don't know. I never knew any."

"Well, I figured you didn't. You don't exactly seem like the fatherly type. Which is why I didn't tell you about her," she said, leaning against the counter and yawning. "Really, it's fine if you want to leave."

"If I wanted to leave, I would've left already," I said to her, standing up and walking beside her. I grabbed a nugget, shoved it in my mouth, chewed a couple times, and swallowed. "You think I care? I'm easy-going. I can usually put up with a hell of a lot of shit."

She shrugged. "First of all, my daughter's *not* 'shit', and I don't need someone to 'put up' with her. She's a lot more important to me than any relationship I could possibly have right now. So if you're just tolerating her in hopes that once I put her to bed, you're going to get a little booty call . . ." She gave me an *oh well!* look. "You're out of luck. Because I'm not doing that with her here. Even when she falls asleep."

I laughed. Even though I would've loved to get in her pants right then, I wasn't some freak who couldn't keep it in mine. "Jesus. I'm so glad you think so much of me."

"Well, I don't know. I haven't been with anyone since the divorce was final," she said, looking down at her lap sheepishly. "Over a year ago. So I don't know how these things work. But I never told you about Alena because I thought I didn't have to. I thought we were just a one-night stand."

"That ain't fair. We've been together twice, now. And I'm here again. You're the one who didn't answer my texts."

"I had a good reason not to!" she said, turning on the water and shoving the pots in the sink. She grabbed the dishwashing soap and squeezed it out onto the dirty dishes.

I stood up as she angrily started to scrub them and leaned on the counter next to her. "You gonna tell me what it is?"

She gave me a scowl. "I think you should already know."

I raised my eyes to the ceiling, thinking. "Nope. No clue."

She scrubbed so hard bubbles flew between us. "You've got to be kidding me. How can you talk about fairness when you've been lying to me?"

My eyes narrowed. "I've never lied to you." I motioned to the pot. "You keep scraping that thing you're gonna end up with a hole in the bottom of it."

She noticed what she was doing and rinsed it off, then dropped it in the drying rack. "So you're going to deny that you know my ex-husband?"

That was something I hadn't expected. Whatever words I'd planned to say to her died in my throat.

"Your . . .what?" It suddenly dawned on me, just who she was talking about. "What's his name?"

"Viktor."

Fuck. Well, now it all made sense. Except the part that put Viktor and Sasha together. Other than accents, they had nothing in common. That big shit had been with my hot girl? Fuck. "Are you telling me that big ugly fuck is your husband?"

"My *ex*-husband. Did he hire you to spy on me?"

I was still trying to process the two of them together when she threw that accusation at me, taking me completely by surprise.

"What? No. Fuck. I didn't know you two were together. Honest, Sasha. The first time I saw you was when you came to The Wall. And I met him for the first time a couple days after that."

She eyed me closely, as if she didn't believe me. "So you're saying it's just a coincidence? How do you know him?"

I dragged my hands down my face. "He works with the club I belong to. That's all. Yeah. It's a coincidence."

Her unforgiving glare didn't waver, like she was waiting for me to crack. She looked a little like her ex-husband, completely emotionless.

Maybe I should've had a flash of pride, knowing I'd fucked the hell out of Viktor's ex-wife, but instead, all I felt was angry that he'd had her before me. A picture started to leak into my mind . . . the two of them together. But it quickly fell apart before it could materialize. Sasha was way too passionate, and Viktor? He was like a wall. Hell, I *couldn't* picture them together.

Alena squealed in the other room. "So let me get this straight. Viktor is your ex, and . . ." I motioned down the hall.

She nodded. "Yes. He's Alena's father. We share custody."

Holy fuck. I stared at her, trying to get it through my head. Because something about it didn't seem right. Sure, they were both Russian, but that was where their similarities ended. That *that* humorless, emotionless fuck could be married to beautiful Sasha, and the father of that cute, tiny little kid?

No. I wouldn't be able to get that through my head. That ugly son of a bitch couldn't have been that lucky.

Chapter Eighteen

Sasha

I watched him trying to process the whole thing, and one thing hit me, as clear as day: He wasn't lying. He really didn't have any idea that I'd been married to Viktor.

They'd worked together. All right. That was fine. Viktor said he had a lot of associates. But I had the feeling whatever Zain's business was, it might not have been strictly legal. So, what, exactly, was Viktor up to? He'd always been so closed-off about his business dealings. All I knew was that it was his family business, he traveled a lot, and that he made deals with various clients. He called it consulting. Consulting on what? I didn't know.

Truthfully, from the way he'd dressed to the people he kept company with, I'd often gotten the feeling that he was involved in the *bratva*. "Your club works with them? And what do they do?"

He stared at me for a long time, hands on his thighs. It was about the same response I'd have gotten from Viktor, all the times I asked him.

I threw up my hands. "It's illegal?"

He nodded. "Technically. We lift cars. We sell them at a premium to a contact overseas, who ships them to Russia for us."

I listened to him, all the while shaking my head. That sounded dangerous. And one thing that asshole had told me, when I had asked him what he did for a living? That it wasn't going to put Alena in danger.

"And what does Viktor do, as part of this scheme?"

"His job is to ensure that nobody fucks with his associate overseas, and that business keeps running smoothly."

"And so if someone gets in the way and starts *fucking* with his *associate*? What does he do to them? He doesn't just *talk* to them, I take it?"

Zain crossed his thick arms over his chest. "You're asking if he kills people. He does. From what I understand, he's a hit-man."

I staggered backwards, feeling for the chair. When I found it, I sank into it, leaning over and burying my face in my hands. Viktor, the man I'd known almost my entire adult life . . . was in the business of killing people. I'd had the suspicion it was something like that, but now that it was out . . . I wanted to scream. I wanted to cry. But most of all, I wanted to rip Viktor's fucking head off.

Consulting, my ass. He was a contract killer.

I blinked, trying to understand. My daughter's father killed people for a living. He'd murdered people to put food on our table. "Oh, my God."

How could Viktor keep this from me? He said he was taking care of me. Was he really? Killing people to provide us with a life? That sounded so backward. So foul.

Zain knelt down in front of me and tried to take my hands away. "Hey."

I pulled away from him. "No. You don't get it. He has a daughter. And he's going around killing people. Forget about him. Do you know what kind of danger that could put our child in? The child he supposedly loves? He has joint custody of her, for God's sake."

He nodded. "Yeah. I agree, it's fucked up."

My eyes flashed to his. "And you do it, too? You kill people?"

He frowned and let out a really long sigh. "Not often. But I carry a gun, mostly for protection. I would if I had to. This isn't a fucking fairy-tale, Sasha. There are people in this business that want to do us harm. I wouldn't hesitate to defend myself or anyone who came after my family."

"Your family? You have a family?"

"Yeah. My brothers. From the club. That's all I have. Anyone I care about. They're good people."

I scoffed. "How good can they be in a line of work that kills people?"

"It's kill or be killed, pretty lady."

"So these men would harm us, too? They'd harm Alena?"

He pressed his lips together, then shook his head. "My men? No. Viktor's crew? I have no idea."

"So what is he doing for you? He's taking care of your dirty work, killing people that are getting in the way of your business? Why can't you take care of it yourselves?"

"We've tried. Believe me. We have. The Hell's Fury have been giving us shit for the better part of a year, now. They started out wanting to take our business, but when we put the brakes on that, they went out for our blood. They've been messing with all of my brothers. We retaliate, get ahead, and they regroup and come back, even stronger than before."

I sighed, then looked around at the mess. There were red footprints on the linoleum in the hall, reminding me of the mess that waited for me in the living room. This was just perfect. I didn't think my life could have possibly gotten more screwed up. "He can't know about us, you know."

He nodded slowly.

"Even though it's over. He can't know."

He gave me a doubtful look. "It ain't over."

"Oh, yes it is. It needs to end, now."

He stroked his short beard and contemplated this. "What if I don't want it to be?"

My jaw dropped a little. His eyes had a way of pinning me down and making me want to agree. But I had to stay firm on this. For my sake, his sake, and especially Alena's. "No. You don't seem to understand. We *can't*. If he finds out what we've done, it will be very bad, for both of us."

"You're divorced, aren't you?"

I nodded.

"So what's the problem?" He let out a quick laugh. "What is he, jealous?"

Oh, he had no idea. If he had any idea of what Viktor was capable of, he wouldn't be laughing. "More than just jealousy. First of all, he knows some very powerful people. I don't doubt that if he found out I'd moved on, he'd take me court and sue me for custody, just out of spite for me. And now that I know he's capable of killing people, I don't put it past him, either. He'd destroy you."

He laughed some more, in that sexy way, as I tried to stop my body from responding. "You don't think I can take care of myself?"

"If you could, would he be here working with your club?"

"Ouch! You hurt me!" He said, grabbing his heart.

I knew Zain could hold his own, but Viktor wasn't a man to be trifled with. They were both very dangerous men. Most people wouldn't want to get on their bad side. If the two of them ended up in a fight, it'd be explosive. "I'm not willing to take any chances where Alena's concerned."

And I didn't want either of them to get hurt. Especially because I knew if they did fight, it would be over me.

"Okay, worry about your kid. You don't need to worry about me."

"I'd rather not worry about any of it. Because I know it would be very bad, and I'd hate to know I was the cause of it."

"So that's the reason you were ignoring my calls?" he said, so flippantly, like he didn't believe me.

"I was ignoring your calls because I thought he'd hired you to spy on me. Yes, he's jealous. I ended things a while ago because I couldn't take his controlling me. He doesn't seem to understand that it's over. He's been trying to get back with me, the entire time." I swallowed. "I haven't been with anyone at all because I've been worried what he might say. You're the first."

He smirked, obviously proud of that little victory, that he'd been so irresistible to me. "But if you didn't have Viktor breathing down your neck, you'd have called me back?"

I squinted at him. "Didn't you hear what I said? He could kill you. He *would* kill you, if he knew what we were doing. Once, when we were out to dinner, a man looked at me in a way he didn't like, and he pummeled the guy in the parking lot. That was just for looking, Zain. You've done a lot more than that."

The smirk on his face grew. I bet he was remembering it, just like I'd started to. I fought the heat that crept over my cheeks. I needed to make this point and not let his sexy *everything* sidetrack me.

I looked away and hardened my voice. "Even you being here right now? It's a bad idea. You should go."

He hitched a shoulder. "I ain't worried."

I trudged over to the cabinets and pulled out some paper towels, a scrub brush, and some cleaner. "You should be."

"Let me help you," he said, following me out to the living room.

I was about to tell him not to, that he *really* needed to make himself scarce, just in case Viktor was spying on me, but then I saw the state of the living room again and realized I needed the help. I handed him the brush. "All right. But after this, you need to go. Let me get some water."

We spent the better part of the next hour on our hands and knees, scrubbing. I put on some classic rock and got him a beer. As we worked, he told me a little about the motorcycle club he belonged to, and what his dealings had been with Viktor. So far, they'd only met each other two or three times, and I got the feeling he'd rubbed Zain the wrong way. Didn't surprise me in the least.

"So, this motorcycle club?" I asked him, curious. "You and your brothers just go around, taking things that don't belong to you and selling them for profit?"

He cocked a grin at me. "Pretty much. And we hang out. Shoot the shit. Do fundraisers for

250

underprivileged kids. Go on long rides together. Every single one of those men . . .they're like my family. Which is good 'because I don't have anyone else."

I sighed. "I hate being alone, not having anyone to rely on. I think about my family in Russia all the time but they married me off and wiped their hands of me. They would be so disappointed, and I'd be so humiliated, if they knew what happened."

He raised an eyebrow. "You never told them you got the divorce?"

I shook my head. "We had a bit of a falling out before Alena was born. They were upset with me because Viktor had told them I was giving him trouble, wanting to take English lessons and finish my paralegal certificate. My mother was very traditional. She told me that as Viktor's wife, my job was to be his whore in the bedroom and spend the rest of my time in the kitchen. I disagreed."

"Holy shit." He laughed. Fucking and cooking? What fucking century are they from?"

251

"Right?" I was happy he agreed with me on this. "So, I told them to mind their own business, and I haven't spoken to them in almost five years. I know they'd be furious if they found out I'm raising their granddaughter as a single mother. Viktor threatened to tell them, but I don't think he has told them anything."

He threw the sponge in the bucket. "Shit, girl. You really have been alone, haven't you? And with that walking tornado in there? I wouldn't just need mental help. I'd probably be locked in a fucking asylum by now."

I smiled at the validation. "She's not always this crazy," I said, pointing at the room. The beige carpet was now a nice shade of pink, the once-white walls were also kind of pink, too. "You just caught her on an off-day."

"Riiight." It was clear from his tone of voice that he didn't believe me.

"Okay, yeah. She's been acting out more and more. I think it's because whenever she goes to Viktor's house, he ignores her. I know he loves her. He just doesn't know how to show it. Especially to a little girl."

"I noticed. The guy seems to be a robot with only one button: Extreme Asshole Mode."

I started to shake my head, but he was right. Viktor had gradually become completely charmless and emotionless. "I guess that's what happens when you kill people for a living."

I had a kink in my back from hunching over, so I arched it and rubbed down low.

"I just wish he didn't have to take it out on her. Oh, he doesn't hit us or anything. I don't think he ever would. But the reason Alena was scared of you? Him. Whenever she sees a man, she gets scared. It was like living with a time bomb. We never could anticipate what would set him off and get him angry."

"Hell," he said. "I'm sorry."

We spent the rest of the time, talking about trivial stuff. We discussed what we liked to do for fun. His answer? Play pool, fix his bike, and hang with his brothers. My answer? Read and continue my schooling. We discussed what we wanted to do when we grew up—he said he just wanted to bike around the country and see the sights; I told him I thought about going to law school so I could get a better career. When I asked him where he thought he'd be in fifteen years, he said, hanging out, doing the same shit. I told him I wanted to get Alena into Harvard.

So basically, where I had ambition, he had no plans for his life other than just to hang out and take things day by day. I was a little shocked at how relaxed he was about everything. Viktor was so Type A, especially when it came to money. But honestly? Zain's laid-back style complemented my own. I'd always felt like I was wound tighter than a wristwatch. Being with Zain made me feel like I could breathe.

"Aren't you worried about running out of time to do the things you want to do?" I asked him.

He laughed. "Yeah. I was. I always thought I'd have all the time in the world to get where I wanted to go. But I'm exactly where I want to be, with my family, my place in the world. I love my life. I enjoy every day. And I sure as hell don't want to spend whatever days I have doing something I don't love. Life's too damn short for that."

I stared at him, thinking. I like being a paralegal, but I didn't know if I loved it. What I loved was being a mom, but I found I couldn't do that well with Viktor constantly berating me. As I watched Zain work, I realized I envied him. I envied that he was so happy and relaxed with who he was and his place in the world.

It was attractive as hell. It made me want to tackle him, right there, on the living room floor and suck up some of his confidence.

Somehow, I resisted. When we were nearly finished, I threw the brush into the bucket of blood-red water and looked at my hands. They were bright red, the pads of my fingers wrinkled. I was sweaty and dirty and probably looked like hell. "Goodness. I need a shower," I said, looking down at my clothes.

His ears perked up, and he gave me that sexy smile.

"That wasn't an invitation," I said to him, cocking an eyebrow at him.

He snapped his fingers. "Damn."

He looked so irresistibly cute like that, on his knees in my living room, grinning like a little boy. After watching the muscles of his arms bulging as he worked out the stains in the carpet for a good hour, I'd hoped the shower would cool me down from the dirty things I was thinking.

But it'd have to wait. Not even until Alena went to bed. Indefinitely.

I refused to have another man sleep under the same roof as Alena until I was absolutely sure I could trust him, and knew she trusted him, too. Maybe not until we were engaged. I was adamant about that. I'd heard the horror stories, and despite Viktor always accusing me of being a bad mother, I'd made a vow. Alena would *always* come first.

I checked the clock. It was nearly eight. I stood up and let out a groan as I brushed the grime off my skirt. "I'd better get her into bed."

I went down the hall to Alena's bedroom. She was on the bed, lying under the blankets, reading books with a flashlight. I lifted the sheets off her head and felt the heat radiating from her body. "How can you breathe like that?"

"Dunno," she said as I smoothed down her hair. It was dry now, but the unruly curls were everywhere. She had all of her princess dolls under there with her, lined up on her pillow. "Who's that boy?"

"That . . . boy?" I pointed to the door.

She nodded, gripping her princess dolls in her tiny hands and moving them off the pillow so I could straighten her little body among them.

"Oh. Nobody really. He's just a friend of mine. Why? You don't like him? Did he scare you?"

"No. I'm not scared of anything, mommy," she said as I tried to tuck her in, lifting up Elsa and Anna. "Wait."

I stopped. "What's the problem? Did you brush your teeth?" That was the usual thing she forgot.

"Yes, of course. And I used the potty, too. I just didn't introduce that boy to Elsa."

I blinked. I didn't think she wanted to see him. Yes, she said she wasn't scared, but she often did that, and then came running to sleep in my bed in the middle of the night. "I can bring him in, if you'd like to do the introductions?"

She sat up in bed and smoothed her hair out. What a little heartbreaker. "Yes, please, Mommy."

I went out to the living room, where Zain was still working on a stubborn part of the carpet. "You've been summoned."

His brow wrinkled.

I pointed down the hall. "I advise you not to wait. She can get bossy."

He jumped to his feet and headed down the hallway. I stood behind him as he said, in a gentler, but still extremely sexy voice, "You wanted me?"

He went deeper into the room and I followed, leaning on the doorjamb as Alena sat up in her bed. "This is Queen Elsa. Elsa, this is . . ."

"Zain," he said, taking the doll's plastic hand between his thumb and forefinger and shaking it a little. "Hey, how are you? Nice dress."

Alena sighed. "She's a queen, so you really have to bow."

"Sorry." He dipped his head. "Better?"

Alena ran a scrutinizing eye over him and finally nodded as she lifted another doll from the pile. "This, here, is Tiana. She's a princess who used to be a waitress."

I watched for at least a half-hour, as my daughter introduced him to every one of her forty-three dolls. Viktor never would've had taken the time for this.

But Zain? He knelt there at her bedside, very quietly and respectfully, and shook the tiny plastic hand of every single one of them.

Alena was clearly in heaven.

And I was right there beside her.

I couldn't help it. It brought more than a few tears to my eyes.

Chapter Nineteen

Zain

Who the fuck knew there were that many princesses and queens in the world? Really, someone should've gotten Disney to shut that shit down.

Still, by the end of it, I think Alena wasn't quite so scared of me anymore. So, all in all, progress. And who knew kids were kind of funny? They really weren't so bad.

When I turned around, Sasha quickly flitted past me, telling her daughter it was past her bedtime and turned off the light, but I was pretty sure before the room went dark, I saw tears in Sasha's eyes.

So that was probably why, when we left the darkened room and went back down the hallway, she grabbed my hand, stood on her toes, and gave me a kiss on the cheek. "Thanks for that."

"For what?"

"For paying attention to her. You didn't have to. But she clearly likes you," she said, holding my hand in both of hers. "Didn't you notice? You're a natural."

I laughed. "Well, I've always had that kind of reputation with the ladies."

"Oh, have you?" she teased. "I hadn't noticed."

We went back out to the living room. The place was clean—or at least, as clean as it was going to get, from the number that little rascal had done on it. I grabbed the bucket, brought it to the sink, and emptied it out. When I finished cleaning it, I turned.

And looked at Viktor's gorgeous ex-wife.

I still couldn't believe that one. But now it kind of made sense. He was used to bullying people and putting them under his control, and he'd controlled her. I could tell from the fear in her eyes every time I mentioned his name. He'd had her under his thumb. It was amazing she'd been able to get herself free. I gave her a lot of credit for that. But something kept her from pulling away from him altogether.

Alena.

"I should go," I said to her, grabbing my helmet.

"Okay," she said, walking me toward the door. "Zain . . ."

I turned to her. She looked so small standing there; I couldn't even imagine her with that big dick of a man. He was the kind of guy I wanted to protect her from. His temper was out of control. And she lived in a crazy world. I could only imagine what it must be like when his temper boiled over.

"Can I call you?" I asked.

She shook her head slowly and gave me a sheepish look. "I don't think it's a good idea."

Somehow, I knew that was coming. "Because of Viktor?"

"Yeah. Because of Viktor."

There to save the Cobras or not, that fuckhead was turning out to be a real thorn in my side. First he went and controlled my club, and now I found out he was throwing a wrench into the thing I had going on with the first girl who actually could have had some sticking-power. I gritted my teeth. "He shouldn't be telling you who you can and can't date, Sasha."

"Yeah, but . . ." she looked up at me with those sad brown eyes and shifted from side to side. "I care about you, Zain. I don't want you to get tangled up in this."

"What if I wanted to be?" I leaned in close to her. Even with all the shit from the day—her long hours at work, the paint that little rascal had thrown on her, the smell of cleanser lingering on her skin—she was still something I wanted to pin against the wall and eat whole.

She shook her head. "Trust me. You don't. Viktor doesn't forgive. And it could ruin everything. We're not just talking about me losing custody of Alena. He wouldn't just turn on you; he'd turn on your club. He's vindictive. Are you willing to risk everything you have?"

"I ain't gonna. All I know is that right is right. And he can't go around controlling people and getting away with it. He needs to learn a lesson or two about the Steel Cobras. Believe me, if he learns, it'll help you and the club."

"I don't think he can be taught. And he can destroy everything, Zain. It's too risky."

I searched her eyes. "I don't want to hurt you or Alena. Will you trust me?"

She drew her lower lip under her teeth. "What do you—"

I took her face in my hands and drew her close to me, setting a quick, dry kiss on her lips. "Just trust me, and I'll take care of Viktor. All right?"

Her eyes widened. "You're not going to tell him about us, are you?"

"No. Of course not."

She gave me a worried look, unsure what I had in mind. Hell, I wasn't sure what I had in mind, either. But I wasn't willing to let her go like this. There had to be more. And I was going to figure out what it was.

I went down the rickety steps outside the building, to where the neon signs from Chow Fun Chinese Restaurant flickered on the broken sidewalks. People were still dining inside, and as I hit the pavement, someone walked out with a bag of take-out. The smell of Chinese food made my mouth water, especially since I hadn't eaten anything but that one burned nugget all day.

I had her taste on my mouth, instead. God, what I wouldn't have given to take her to bed and feast on her all night long. I got that she was trying to look out for her daughter. I respected that, but hell . . . tearing myself away from her was damn hard.

That thought lodged in my head, I kick-started my Harley and headed toward my house. As I drove, still thinking of Sasha and her cute little kid and wondering how the fuck I'd ever get them out from under Viktor's control, I glanced in one of my rear-view mirrors and saw the single headlight of a bike on my tail.

I quickly made a turn onto Sunset, and the bike followed.

ZAIN

Not a big deal. There were tons of bikers in
Aveline Bay, and because the weather of late had been
perfect, a lot of people went on motorcycle rides.
People were always passing through here, taking a
scenic ride up the coast.

But when I turned down a narrower street, and
the bike kept on my ass, I started to wonder.

Squinting at the mirror and adjusting my helmet,
I noticed the denim kutte as the bike went under the
yellow glow of the streetlamp. The guy had big guns,
covered in tattoos. But I knew my brothers. I would've
recognized who it was if he was one of ours. Plus, they
knew better than to hang behind me like that.

I revved the engine and sped up.

So did the guy behind me. He ended up right on
my tail.

I made a quick right and pulled into an alley as I
saw the guy reaching into his waistband and pulling out
a gun.

Fucking hell.

Thinking fast, I took the first right I could find, then another quick right, into a narrow, dark alley. I slowed to a fast stop and jumped from the bike before it'd even stopped moving. Once I did, I pulled the gun from the seat compartment, where I kept it, leveling it at the bike just as it approached.

I got off one shot, which must've scared the fucker, because he pulled up off his seat and gunned his motorcycle, speeding off into the night.

I jogged out to follow him, leveling my gun at his back. As he passed under another streetlight, I saw the patch. The flames. Hell's Fury.

Exhaling with relief, I went back to my bike, shaking my head. What the fuck were those assholes doing out here?

I stiffened as a thought occurred to me.

What if they'd seen me at Sasha's? What if I'd led them right to her apartment?

Fucking hell.

The Fury were known for going after people's families. As a former prospect who decided to turn tail on them and their Public Enemy Number One, since they couldn't get to me, the people I held dear were next on the list. Up until now, I hadn't had anyone like that.

But now . . .

The last thing I needed was to get Sasha roped into the Hell's Fury situation.

I needed to talk to Viktor. As soon and as fast as I could.

EVIE MONROE

Chapter Twenty

Sasha

The following morning I woke to a perfect day. Warm and beautiful, without a cloud in the sky. The weather that I loved so much about living in California.

Even so, before I rose from my bed, I looked up at the ceiling, my insides roiled with worry. Worry for Viktor, for having gotten himself into this dangerous lifestyle. Worry for Zain, for seeming so gung-ho on challenging him. And of course, worry for Alena, because I'd brought her into this turbulent situation.

How could I have known Viktor was up to no good? Yet, maybe I should have known. There'd always been rumors going around town that he was part of the Russian mafia. His mother had been dead for many years before I met him, and when I was in the process of moving to America, his father died. He'd told me before that his father had trained him and left him the contacts for his family business, but he never said what they were.

It was my own fault, for just accepting his word at face value. I'd been too hopeful that Viktor would be my dream come true. That had made me blind to all the signals. And as more of the façade of us as a happy family started to crumble, I ignored the signs, scared to realize the truth. He'd kept an entire room in our condo locked and secret from me, but if I'd really wanted to, I could've found the key.

The thing was, I didn't want to. I wanted to live in ignorant bliss and pretend. Because he was all I had.

And now? Zain seemed hell-bent on confronting Viktor, and that could only be bad news. For all of us.

This was all my fault.

Alena usually got up with the sun. This morning, I dressed, pig-tailed, and gave her Eggos two hours before I had to report for work, so I decided to take her to the playground down the street before daycare. After slipping on a blue dress for work, I scuffed into my sneakers instead of my heels and took her hand. We sang Polly Put the Kettle On as we made our way out the door.

Outside, the stale stench of old Chinese food hung heavy in the air. We walked along the busy main street, past ethnic food market and the taco place and the small hardware store that never had any customers—to a small, wooded park with an old jungle gym, seesaw, merry-go-round, and swing set.

"Come on," I said to her, squeezing her chubby little hand as I looked around the mostly-empty park, shivering a little in the morning chill. "Let me push you on the swings."

She ran for the red swing, oblivious to the homeless people sleeping on the benches. She jumped onto the swing and dangled her tiny little legs as she pushed off.

As happy as she was, I was hyper-aware as I scanned the area, half-expecting Viktor to show up and grab me by the back of the neck, hissing, *I know what you've been up to, solnyshka.*

His sunshine. What a joke. Sunshine exists regardless of human interference. He had to realize that his mere presence was dimming my light, and had been, ever since he issued his first demand.

"Wee! This is fun!" Alena shrieked with glee, breaking me from my reverie. Alena had such a strong, powerful light. And maybe, if her father didn't change, her light would dim, too.

I shuddered at that thought.

As I pushed her, she worked her little legs, trying to get up the right swinging rhythm. "Mommy. Is your friend coming over tonight?"

I sighed. I'd thought about him the entire night, alone, in my bed, but this time, I wasn't thinking about the sex. I was thinking about that wonderful feeling of having a man's arms around my body. At one time, very long ago, I could remember nestling into the warmth of Viktor's arms and feeling protected. He was so strong and powerful, I felt like nothing or no one could harm me.

It'd been a long time since I felt protected, but oh, how I wanted to feel it again.

I wanted to feel it with Zain.

But once bitten, twice shy. How could I have known the very person protecting me would wind up being my biggest threat?

That kind of safety I dreamed of seemed impossible. Zain had told me not to worry about Viktor, but I didn't believe him. How could he possibly get Viktor to change? Jealousy and a bad temper were in his blood.

"I don't think so, sweetheart," I said, pushing her harder.

"Oh. Too bad. I liked him. He was funny."

She liked him. And here, she'd spent most of the evening giving him dirty looks. I laughed. Kids were funny.

"He was, wasn't he?" I replied, smiling fondly at the image of Zain kneeling down at her little toddler bed and trying his best to humor her. It was definitely the type of moment that would make a woman's ovaries explode.

A few minutes later, Alena tired of the swings and pointed excitedly to the merry-go-round. I tried to talk her out of it on other trips to the park. I'd seen kids get hurt when the centrifugal force threw them to the ground if they were too small to hold on tight.

"Oh, please, Mommy," she pleaded, so I said, okay, figuring I could control the speed. She hopped on and I told her not to let go as I started to spin the old thing. It creaked loudly as it turned, and Alena shrieked with joy.

"Oh, mommy, I'm getting dizzy!" she said, her big blue eyes going wild.

I laughed at her, then looked up and noticed something in the distance that alarmed me. Rather, someone, at the edge of the park, just beyond the trees and the garbage cans.

It was a man on a motorcycle, wearing a helmet, with his face turned toward me.

At first, I thought it was Zain because of the tattoos and bike. He also wore a denim vest with patches on it, and he looked tough, just like Zain. But he was a smaller man, and his bike was different from Zain's.

I stared at him, until I realized Alena was whining that I was going too fast. "Mommy, I can't hold on."

I grabbed the metal bar and skidded along with it to slow it down, reminding myself to pay attention to my daughter. "Oh, sweetheart! Sorry. Are you okay?"

Alena gave me a big smile, then peeled herself off the platform once the merry-go-round had come to a stop. She wobbled around dizzily, reaching for me to steady her.

"Whoa," I said, gathering her in my arms.

"Are you okay? Breathe. Relax."

And then like the little adventurer she was, her face lit up and she said, "That was fun. More."

Checking my phone, I shook my head when I saw the time. "Sorry, *mishka*. I think we should go."

"Oh, please, mommy! Five more minutes."

I sighed. The girl had a way of making me the biggest pushover. And we did have the time. Besides, getting into work early hadn't done me any favors lately. "Okay. We can stay a few more minutes."

She rushed over to the seesaw and sat on the low end that was buried in a patch of yellow grass. "Come on, Mommy! Get on with me."

Seesaws don't work when one person is heavy and one person is a lightweight little girl, but I hiked my skirt up to mid-thigh and slipped on.

I did my best to bounce her up and down, until she got bored, and I sensed she was about to get off. Anticipating her flight, I quickly dug my sneakers into the ground to avoid falling on my ass and swung my leg over so we both got off without mishaps.

When I looked back at the spot where I'd seen the motorcycle, the man had disappeared. I checked around to see if he'd gone somewhere else, but I couldn't see him anywhere.

What did that mean? Was that someone else from Zain's club? And if so, why was he following me? I had to admit, I really didn't know what a motorcycle club was all about, but I knew that Zain wasn't involved in the most legal of things. As if I didn't have enough to worry about. I didn't want Alena getting wrapped up in anything dangerous. I'd told that to Viktor a million times. And for me to lead her into the same danger, with Zain?

No, it wasn't good. I told him I didn't want to see him again.

I needed to stick to that.

No matter what my body was telling me.

"Come on, Alena," I said. I took her hand and led her out of the park. "We've got to get you to daycare."

We walked back the way we'd come, toward the apartment. As we reached an intersection, a motorcycle suddenly streaked by, out of nowhere. Shocked, we both took a few steps back. Alena let out a piercing cry. I watched it zoom away, too stunned to yell at the jerk. His back to me, I noticed the vest he was wearing had flames on it, not cobras like Zain's. So that meant he had to be from a different club.

I wished I knew. And what the hell was he doing here, this early in the morning? Had he been following me?

Whatever it was, by the time I got back to the apartment, I'd convinced myself it was a very good thing that I'd told Zain we couldn't continue seeing each other. The problem with me was that I was looking for safety and security in all the wrong places. Viktor? Mistake. Zain? Also a mistake. I needed to find someone I trusted. Someone who would love us both and insure neither of us got hurt in the process.

We climbed up the stairs past the Chinese restaurant, and I quickly changed into my heels, gathered up my purse, car keys, and Alena's princess backpack and lunch. I locked up the apartment and hurried us to my car.

As I strapped Alena in and settled her with her Princess Belle book to occupy her on the ride. I loved watching her try to sound out the letters she'd recently learned and knit her little brow as her eyes went over the words. As cute as she was, I couldn't avoid noticing she had the shape of Viktor's eyebrows with that same high arch.

I kissed her forehead, then closed the door and got in the driver's seat.

Yes, Zain had been good with Alena. But that was only one time. And yes, I had a feeling he was a man of his word. But he was involved in bad things and getting involved with a guy so inherently dangerous could lead to trouble. What if giving my heart to him was as big a mistake as I'd made with Viktor?

As I looked into the rearview mirror at my darling daughter, it occurred to me that some of the best things in my life had come from my biggest mistakes.

EVIE MONROE

Chapter Twenty-One

Zain

The following afternoon, I went to the clubhouse to find Viktor there, lounging in a chair, his legs spread wide and his nose buried in his cell phone. He had his jacket off, and was wearing a shoulder holster, a gun strapped to his side. Fucking big man, really thought he was something special.

Just the thought of him in bed with Sasha made me sick to my stomach. I had to wonder if he'd made her come. If she ever loved him. What the fuck had he done, what kind of wool had he pulled over her eyes to make her think he was worthy of her?

The fact that he would control her like that? Pissed me off even more.

But I'd promised her I wouldn't tell Viktor about us, and I intended to stick to my word.

Still, I didn't think I could stick to Cullen's play-nice credo. Hell, no. I didn't care if this guy was going to save all of our asses from the Hell's Fury. We didn't need him, a low-life asshole who thought he could treat women like shit in order to feed his own ego. We'd deal with the Fury on our own, if need be.

If my stance on that ended up getting me ousted from the Cobras, so be it.

But I had a feeling, once my brothers knew what this asshole had been up to, they'd back me up.

I grabbed a couple beers from the fridge. "So," I said, sidling up to him. I slid one of the beers over to him. "What's new, Viktor?"

I couldn't keep the menace out of my voice. He looked up at me, his blue eyes narrowed in suspicion. "What do you want?" he growled.

"I asked you what was new." I pulled out a chair and sat next to him, as if I was his best friend, getting ready for a chat. "What? You not interested in some friendly conversation?"

"I'm doing business," he muttered, his words clipped as he motioned to his phone.

"Well," I said, trying to keep it light. "I got the feeling you and I got off on the wrong foot. And I thought maybe we could clear the air."

He swiped the beer from the table and took a swig. "I'm here to do a job. I don't need to be friends. With anyone."

I nodded. Asshole. "All right. We don't have to be friends. But we can still talk. Shoot the shit. Let each other in on our lives," I said, giving him a smirk. "Me? I've lived in Aveline Bay all my life. What about you? How long you been in this country?"

He peered at me, his face a mask of stone. At first, I thought he wouldn't answer, but then he said, "I came over from Russia when I was sixteen. That is when I became an American citizen."

All right. This was good. "You like America?"

He nodded. "I had nothing in Russia. Here, I am someone."

"Yeah? So . . . you handle many situations like ours? You kill a lot of assholes?"

He raised an eyebrow, and his eyes glinted with pride. "Yes. I go where I'm needed. And I'm good at what I do."

Now I was getting someplace. Time to go in for the kill. "Gotcha. You have a wife? Kids?"

I saw a glimmer of something in his eyes. His face hardened, and he let out a grunt. "No."

I gave him an incredulous look. "Yeah?"

He stared at me, unblinking.

"You sure?" My smirk widened. "Because I met someone who says she knows you. Her name is Sasha. Sasha Kotov. Ever hear of her? Same last name as yours, right?"

That single word broke through the stone on his face, and I finally saw some emotion. Rage. His entire face contorted with it, his pale skin growing red from the tight collar of his shirt. A big purple vein bulged on the side of his face. "What?"

ZAIN

Around the clubhouse I could feel my brothers tensing. Cullen was eyeing me like he knew I was about to create some havoc. I loved every second of it, loved giving the asshole his due. "You heard me."

I opened my mouth to say more, but I didn't need to. He pushed away from the table, the chair skittering backwards and falling over, and advanced on me. Faster and nimbler than him, I easily skirted away as he growled, "You know Sasha?"

I laughed and scratched my temple nonchalantly. "Pretty well, actually. She's a sweet girl. Hot, too. Really hot."

He charged me so fast that this time I couldn't get away. He grabbed my t-shirt, twisting the fabric in his fist. I let him, because hell, I was having enough fun as it was, just watching him squirm. His voice was low. "Tell me how you know her."

"Zain!" Cullen called behind the wall of a man in front of me. "Cut it out."

Hilarious, considering the guy had me by the shirt. I could've leveled this guy with one punch if I wanted, but in the interest in not fucking up the plans Cullen was working out to remove the Hell's Fury, I resisted. I shoved him off me. "I guess you could say we're friends. Yeah, good friends."

"I don't fucking believe that's all you are," he gritted out, trying to push me back against the wall.

I blocked him and shouldered him hard, making him stagger back. "I guess you'll just have to take my word for it," I said, winking at him. "But I'll tell you one thing. That daughter of yours . . . what's her name? Alena? She sure is cute as a button. So that's why it's sad to hear that you seem to have forgotten all about that family of yours. They wouldn't like to hear that."

The rage in his eyes reignited.

I turned to leave and the next thing I knew, he'd grabbed me by the collar of my kutte, yanking me backwards.

When I turned, I anticipated the swing and ducked. I got off a side punch of my own in his ribs, and then a straight shot, on the side of his square jaw.

It didn't move him at all, but he did reach over and massage his chin, checking his fingertips for blood. There was none, but his tongue worked inside his cheek, probably tasting it. Maybe I'd rearranged a couple of his teeth. "You're a fucking dead man!" he screamed.

"Jesus fucking Christ!" Cullen muttered as Viktor charged me, his shoulders and all his three hundred pounds of solid muscle hitting me in the abdomen. He backed me all the way up to the wall. I blocked his shot, but I was cornered. As close to dead meat as I'd ever been.

But I wasn't worried. When it came to fighting, I had ego, because it was deserved. I didn't lose. Didn't matter how big the asshole was. And yeah, Viktor was a lot bigger than me, but all I had to do was imagine his massive body on top of Sasha's. It would've filled my fists with enough white-hot power to pummel him into nothing more than a splotch on the ground.

Hart and Drake ran to the fight, trying to pull him off me, but I didn't need them. I held my own, blocking his punches and delivering some of my own . . . smiling the whole time. It brought me nothing but joy to get this asshole riled.

"Holy shit just stop it, assholes," Nix said. I could see frustration replacing the blind rage in Viktor's eyes. He kept going for the kill punch, and I kept blocking him and getting in shots of my own. I'd gotten in a good one, right in his nose, and now he was bleeding from both nostrils. Me? This was just a walk in the park for me. A little sweat, and a little heavy breathing, but this was just a nice workout.

Nix and Jet got into it, finally getting between us. When Nix threw his body in the middle of things and Cullen finally said, "Hey. Now. Stop it," Viktor's eyes finally fell on him.

He shoved me and backed away, adjusting his tie. "I don't need this bullshit. You hear me?"

Then he turned on his heel, grabbed his phone and briefcase from the place where he'd set them, and stalked toward the door.

Good.

My brothers didn't look very happy, though. Cullen wasn't one to get worried about things, but even I had to say, he looked as close to concerned as I'd ever seen him.

"Wait, where are you going?" he called after Viktor as the asshole reached the door and yanked it open with force.

"I'm leaving. The deal's off," he growled bluntly.

"Hold on," Cullen said, giving me the stink-eye and heading off after him. He ran out the door, but a second later, returned, raking his hands through his hair. "He's fucking driven off. Great. *Great!* Do you even want to be in this fucking club, Zain?"

It wasn't often I saw Cullen so riled. I gloated over my win for about three more seconds, but then Cullen's eyes fell on me, hard and accusing, and I started feeling like he wanted me to feel. Like shit.

"Jesus Christ, Zain. You want to destroy the Cobras? Is that what you want?"

I didn't answer. I was still holding on to that little sliver of smugness for getting the best of that wife-abusing motherfucker. But the more Cullen waited, urging me to answer, the more of it trickled away.

"Well?" he said, coming over to me and crossing his arms, waiting for my explanation. He got right in my face so I had to look at him. He was known for being one calm fucker, but now, I could feel the anger coming off him in hot waves.

I shrugged. "Well what?"

He looked about ready to punch me himself. "What the fuck was that little display for? Answer me! You really want to bury the Cobras? Is that it?"

I shook my head.

"No? Are you sure, fucker?" He shoved me in the chest. "Because that's what it looked like back there!"

I looked beyond him, and a couple of my other brothers—Hart, getting another beer, and Nix, just staring at me like he backed up Cullen's every word and hated the hell out of me. Yeah, they were my brothers, but there was one thing that mattered more than brothers. The Cobras themselves. And I guess I'd just gone and shit all over them.

Not to mention, I'd promised Sasha I wouldn't do what I'd just done. I said I wouldn't let Viktor know that I knew Sasha.

But I couldn't help it. I ran right into it. It was like I wanted to fuck that guy up so bad, I didn't care who I had to hurt in order to do it. Sometimes my sense of justice got the better of me. And that guy needed to be put in his place.

But maybe I shouldn't have been the one to do it.

What the fuck was wrong with me? The guy was an asshole. What was I . . . jealous that he he'd had a family with Sasha before me?

No, that was wrong. I didn't want that.

Cullen dragged his hands down his face. "I've just spent the better part of a week getting that man up to speed on our business so that I could convince him that our club was worth fighting for. He'd finally agreed that we needed to make a move, and quick, and you just went and tore apart the whole fucking deal in one minute. Why?"

I hitched a shoulder. "Because—"

"Don't." He held up a hand. "Because whatever answer you have ain't good enough. I don't want to hear it."

I closed my mouth and prepared myself for the rest of his wrath. Instead, he turned away and stalked about three steps before railing on me.

"You're fuckin' his girl, is that it? And you don't like the fact that he got to her first, so you felt you needed to get your digs in. I hope you're Goddamn happy. What a fucking waste."

"Not a waste," I murmured. "He was married to her. He abused her, the whole time they were married. He's an ass—"

"I don't fucking care if he killed her!" Cullen boomed; his eyes full of fire.

That, I never thought I'd hear Cullen say. I never thought I'd hear a Cobra say that. We didn't work that way. "Fine. If that's the way you feel. But I do care. And I know what's right."

He shook his head and a small, ironic smile came over his face. "Good for you. But you don't let it get in front of Cobra business. I don't fucking care if he mass-murdered a thousand women. None of that concerns me, Zain. What does? The Fury, and they're breathing down our necks worse than ever. We had a way of getting out without killing ourselves in the process. He was it. And now he's gone."

I looked over at Nix, who was hanging his head. Not interceding meant he agreed with Cullen. Scanning the other faces of the men, not a single one looked at me. Their silence felt like condemnation.

Maybe I had no one on my side in this.

"Sometimes I think you're still working for the Fury," he muttered, rubbing his eyes. "Sometimes I think you forget what they did to you."

That was wrong. I remembered. I remembered all those months of watching my back, waiting for them to strike, after I'd told them I was done. But I'd deal with it all for the rest of my life rather than fight next to Viktor Kotov.

I didn't care. Right is right. If the Cobras died doing what was right, at least we wouldn't die next to a total scumbag.

"And asshole or not, you will work with him. If I manage to get him back, which I don't even know if it's possible right now."

I thrust my hands into the pockets of my jeans and averted my eyes, ignoring him.

That pissed him off. "You hear me, Zain? In fact, I want you to go and get him back yourself. It's the least you can do for us. Get on your motherfuckin' knees and beg him if you have to. Suck his fuckin' dick. I don't care. I want him on our side. You got that? Or else you're out of this club."

My eyes snapped to his. He couldn't be serious.

He wanted me to go down on my hands and knees in front of Viktor? Suck his dick? Show him what a pussy we were?

Fuck that.

Viktor would just love that. Relish it. He was all for blatant displays of power. I hated that son of a bitch. And no one ever told me to bend over and take anything.

I'd never directly disobeyed an order from my president. But this was one I couldn't carry out. No fucking way.

"Then I guess I'm out," I said coolly, grabbing my helmet and striding to the exit, as something occurred to me.

Viktor was gone. I'd assumed he'd gone to tell his bosses in Russia to end the contract with the Cobras. But . . . more likely . . . what if he'd gone to find Sasha?

Fuck. After what I said, of course, that was where he'd gone. He'd never let her escape after that. And I'd told myself I'd protect her. What the fuck was I doing?

I broke into a run as I headed for the door. I could feel their eyes following me as I pulled open the door and escaped into the light of day. I knew at least one of them would try to stop me, and I was right. A second after I straddled my bike, Nix appeared. "Whoa. Zain. You can't do this."

I fixed my helmet on over my head. "Yeah, I can. And I've got to go."

He gave me an incredulous look. "Wait. Don't."

"I've got somewhere to be. And I can go, Nix. I don't even feel a little bit of remorse because I know it's right. That asshole isn't worth it, and I won't be on the same side as him. I don't care what Cullen says. I'm done."

"You're doing this for a girl?" He gave me an incredulous look and put his hands on my handlebars to stop me.

"Pardon me, but I think every fucking one of you went a little batshit crazy over some woman. Remember Liv? One would think you'd understand."

Right then, he was probably thinking about his girlfriend. He'd found her in the trunk of a car we boosted and holed her up in his apartment to keep her safe from the Fury, against our better judgment. She was pregnant now, due to give birth to his first kid at any moment.

"Maybe we did. But we didn't step out on the Cobras. No woman comes before your brothers."

"Right. Because your brothers had your back. I've had all of your backs, all the fucking time, because I, more than anyone, know what the Fury can do. It's mostly my fault they're on our asses. But you're refusing to have mine when I need you." I got ready to turn on the ignition. "So I'm out."

"Zain—"

I didn't give him a chance to say more. All I could think was that Viktor must've gotten to Sasha by now, and whatever he had to say to her wouldn't be good. I gunned the engine and tore out of the parking lot to find Sasha.

Chapter Twenty-Two

Sasha

The living room of my apartment over the Chow Fun Chinese restaurant looked out onto the main road of Aveline Bay's old downtown. Ever since they built the freeway that bypassed this place, it got very little traffic. Across the street was an old vacuum cleaner store. It had probably closed down twenty years ago, the storefront windows soaped up with a crooked and yellowed AVAILABLE sign. Homeless people sometimes walked up and down the street, panhandling, but it was pretty quiet, except for the occasional motorcycle engine or eighteen-wheeler's air horn blasting through the air from the freeway.

I heard another motorcycle engine as Alena and I were sprawled on the once-tan, now-pink-splotched living room carpet, playing Chutes and Ladders. She was pouting because she'd gotten the long chute that took her nearly to the start of the game.

"Do-over," I said to her as I jumped up from crisscross applesauce and crossed to the window. "I didn't see it. You can spin again."

Normally, this would be a good time to teach her about the merits of being a gracious loser, but after a long day at work, I was too tired.

I didn't have to tell her twice. Excitedly, she flicked the spinner again and continued on her way as I tented the blinds to peer out.

While at work, I'd thought all day about the man on the motorcycle I'd seen while playing with Alena at the playground. It'd distracted me from putting my best foot forward, and Marina had been in such an epically bitchy mood that I'd gotten more than a few dirty looks from her.

I knew that Zain's club had enemies, and just by associating with him, I might be opening myself and Alena up to dangers. When I saw that man this morning, I had to wonder, would they come after me out of spite because of him?

I breathed a sigh of relief when I looked out the front window and saw Zain pulling to the curb on his bike. He yanked off his helmet and strode toward the staircase at the side of the building. A second later, I heard his heavy boots on the cement steps.

I turned to see Alena clapping her hands. "Look, Mommy! I won."

Sure enough, her marker was at the top of the board. "Oh, good!" I said, giving her a hug.

When Alena had asked whether my *friend* was coming over tonight, I'd been happy to say no. I didn't want her to see me getting too close to any man too soon. But after that strange man I'd seen in the morning, I was relieved to have Zain here.

When he knocked, Alena sprang up to answer the door. She pulled it open and let out a bright, "Oh, hi!" hanging on the doorknob, giving him her best eyelash bat.

"How ya doing?" he said to her. "Fist bump?"

She gave him one as I came up behind her. I kissed the top of her head as she said, "Look. Mommy, it's your friend."

His eyes were hot on mine. It made my heart do a little flutter. "So it is. Nice to see you, Zain."

"We were just playing Chutes and Ladders," Alena continued excitedly. Zain must've graduated to her *favorite* people list, because she was either completely bashful and unwilling to say two words to grown-ups she didn't like, or she couldn't shut up around those she loved. There was no in between. "Wanna play with us?"

He shrugged. "Sure. Haven't played in years, so you might have to teach me."

"I will," she said excitedly. "Come on. It's not that hard."

I led him into the living room, and he looked over the game as we all crouched around the game board. We played, the two adults of the group mostly silent, since Alena filled all the gaps in the conversation with rules of game play, observations about life, and a thousand questions for our guest. "What's your favorite animal?" she asked him. "Mine's a dolphin."

His gorgeous eyes lit up. "Dolphins are cool. Yeah. I guess they're my favorite, too."

"What's your favorite color?"

"Blue," he said.

Her jaw dropped. "That's mine!"

"No way. Fist bump."

She excitedly reached across the board to comply. "It's like we're twins!"

When we finished our third game, I told Alena to go in her room and play with her princess coloring books and let me talk to our guest alone. As she scampered off, I caught him watching her, a hint of a smile on his face.

"She's a good kid," he said.

"I know. Why did you come here?" I asked him.

He smirked. "What, you're not happy to see me?"

"It's not that. I could just tell by the look on your face that something was wrong. Did it have to do with Viktor? Did you see him?"

His mouth curled down and he nodded. "Yeah. I did. Unfortunately. And he might know about us."

My blood ran cold. "Wait. What? How?"

His strong face turned just about as sheepish as it possibly could look. "I . . . might have told him."

My jaw dropped. "What? You promised you—"

"I know. But I'll keep you safe."

"That's not the point!" I shouted, throwing up my arms. "I didn't want this complication in my life!"

"I get it. And I'm sorry."

I probably should've been angrier than I actually was. Maybe because I'd never heard Viktor apologize to me for anything. "Are you really?"

"Of course. But he knows he can't mess with me. I promise he won't ever hurt you again." He went to the window and peered out. "That's why I came here. I thought he might be here."

"Oh, he will. Probably. When he's had enough vodka to kill a horse." I buried my face in my hands. "Oh, God."

Zain came over to me and put a hand on my shoulder. "I'll make sure he doesn't."

I shook him away. "You don't get it. You just being here is a problem. He's never laid a finger on me, but I can't put it past him to degrade me in front of Alena and cause a big scene. If you're gone, he's more likely to talk calmly."

"You really think he would?"

I swallowed. No. He'd gone ballistic just thinking I was fucking around with people. If anything could get him to push past his self-imposed limits and lay a finger on me, finding out Zain and I were lovers might be it. "I don't know."

"You really want me to leave?"

"Yes," I said, but instantly regretted it. That was the last thing I wanted. Right now, every fiber of my being wanted him here. "No. I don't know."

"Make up your mind. I'll do whatever you want."

I reached for his hand and tilted his knuckles to the light. I'd seen the purple bruises there before, while he was playing the game, but I didn't say anything then.

"Did you fight him?"

He nodded.

"And?"

He shrugged, looking smug. "He looks worse than I do."

I let out a sigh. "No. Wipe that look off your face, Zain. He may not be the best person on earth but he's that little girl's father!" I pointed down the hall. "They may not have the best relationship on earth, but they do love each other. And if you hurt him, you'll hurt all of us, too. We may be divorced, but because of Alena he'll always be family."

"He abused you, Sasha. Maybe not with his fists but with his words, which can be worse. If you think I can just sit back and let him—"

"Yes. That's what you were supposed to do! It's not your job to save me! I did that myself when I filed for divorce! I can fight my own battles!" I shouted at him, jumping up. "And if—"

"Mommy?"

The fragile voice stopped me cold. I swiveled and saw Alena was standing in the doorway, in her little pink tutu and her scabby knees, watching me with saucer-sized eyes. I'd left Viktor for this very reason. Because I didn't want to subject her to this kind of incessant shouting. Not from me; I was always too afraid to quarrel with him and tell him what I wanted. But Viktor always raised his voice, all the time. And now here I was, shouting at Zain.

God, I must be the worst mother ever.

"Hi, honey. Everything's okay," I said, glaring at Zain as I walked over to her. I grabbed her hand and led her back toward her bedroom at the back of the apartment. "Come on, sweetheart. Let's get you all dressed in your nightgown and ready for bed."

I closed the door and helped her slip on her Ariel nightgown as she stood on top of her bed. "Why were you yelling at that nice man, Mommy?" she asked me.

"I wasn't yelling."

"Yes, you were."

I sighed. "I know, all right, I was. But it's not anything to be concerned about. Like I told you. Grown-ups sometimes disagree. But it wasn't anything for me to get worked up over. I was being silly."

She nodded, too much in agreement.

"Oh, you!" I said, squeezing her fat little cheeks and kissing her as I lifted her up on my hip. I pushed open the door to get her teeth brushed, and the first thing I saw was Zain, at the other end of the hallway, watching me. I skirted past him, into the bathroom, and put bubble gum-flavored toothpaste on her princess toothbrush.

As I handed it to her, I saw his face in the mirror. "I'm sensing a running princess theme," he noted as his eye swept over the Little Mermaid shower curtain.

"You figured that out just now?" I muttered to him, laughing as she finished spitting into the sink. I motioned to her to use the potty and closed the door, which left Zain and I out in the hallway.

He said, "I get it, you can—"

I held up a hand. "Don't. Stop. Whatever you say, you're going to start me yelling again. And I promised I wouldn't do that in front of her."

As the toilet flushed, I pasted that happy smile on my face. She opened the door and eyed me suspiciously. She may have been only four, but she clearly wasn't an idiot.

"Come on," I said to her, as she ran ahead of me and jumped into bed. I pulled the covers up over her, still smiling that goofy smile of hers.

From the look on her face, she definitely didn't buy it.

I ignored it and kissed her forehead.

She looked from between us and said, "You two better make up. My teacher says that even when you don't agree, you should shake hands and make up."

Zain let out a little chuckle and offered me his hand. I shook it, reluctant at first. "Happy?"

She nodded triumphantly.

I settled her into bed and pulled her covers up to her chin. "Good night," I said to her, turning on her nightlight as she hugged Zain tight. I flipped off the light switch and blew her a last kiss good night.

Zain followed me into the living room, and I turned to face him. "What exactly did you tell Viktor?"

"I told him I knew you. And that was all. It was enough. It threw him into a fucking fit," he said with a shrug. "After we fought, he said he wasn't going to help our club and he stormed out."

I raised an eyebrow. "So he's not working with you anymore?"

"I don't know. The president wanted me to go back and make nice with him so he'll help us again. But I told him, in not so blunt terms, to go fuck himself. And now I guess I'm out of the club."

"What? You're out?" I covered my mouth with my hands. "I thought you said you needed him to help you against another club."

"Yeah. I did. But I'm not working with him, Sasha. Not after what he did to you."

I couldn't believe what I'd just heard him say. He'd talked about the club like it was the most important thing in his life. He had a huge tattoo that proved his allegiance. To just give it all up . . . for me? Because he didn't like my ex?

"Can you take it back?"

His eyes snapped to mine. "What?"

"I mean, I know what the club means to you. You can't simply leave it. Don't be crazy, Zain. If the club is your life, then leave me and go do what you have to do. I can take care of myself."

He was quiet for a long time. Then he said, "Maybe I want something else out of life."

His gaze nearly pinned me against the wall. If he kept looking at me like that, I'd lose my every inhibition and wouldn't be able to kick him out. I needed to stop. "I think it's better if you go now. I can't have you being here if Viktor shows up."

He came closer to me. "Did you hear me?"

I nodded. Yes, I heard him, but I was doing my best to ignore it.

"I want you more than the club," he murmured, taking my chin in his hand and stroking my cheek with the pad of his thumb. His eyes scoured my face, so super-heated I felt like I might burst into flames. "Tell me you don't want me, too."

I swallowed and tried to shake my head, but he kept me steady there, against the wall.

"Tell me you're not falling for me, and I'll leave."

I couldn't lie. I couldn't say what I desperately wanted to, to stop this and keep Alena and me safe. I closed my eyes to block him out, but I could still feel him everywhere. Desire pooled hot in my belly.

Finally, I whispered, "I want you, Zain."

His hand slid around my neck, drawing me up to his level. He licked at the seam of my lips, priming me, nibbling softly as I let out a little moan. He was such a good kisser—for all his strength and power, he kissed me gently, like he wanted to cherish me. It felt so good that I could just stand there, kissing him all day. Yes, I was definitely falling for him.

Falling for him so fast and hard that I'd nearly abandoned my own rules.

"Wait," I said, nudging him away. "We can't do this. Alena . . ."

"All right." He took my hand and started to lead me to the sofa.

I shook my head. "No. You need to—"

He silenced me with another kiss, and then I completely lost it. I stopped thinking about him leaving, because I never could let that happen, and started wondering how I could survive this night without putting Alena in any jeopardy.

Still holding his hand, I pulled him toward the bedroom. "You're not staying the night. You're leaving before she wakes up. You understand me?"

He nodded, but I really didn't know if he did understand. I didn't care, at that point. I needed him, more than I'd ever needed anything in my life.

Chapter Twenty-Three

Zain

Sure, I'd done some stupid, rash things before in my life. And by the time I'd gotten to Sasha's house, I'd thought my telling Cullen to fuck off and storming out on my brothers was going to go down in history as the worst one ever.

But the second Sasha closed the door and put her hands on me, everything about me leaving the Cobras was forgotten. And I was hers.

Pressing her against the door of her bedroom, I lifted her dress to her armpits, baring her tiny panties and her beautiful tits to me. I leaned down, sucking on each nipple in turn, listening to the small sounds of pleasure she made as I peaked each nipple to a diamond point. Then, I knelt in front of her, putting my hands on those full hips of hers, kissing her tight abdomen and running my tongue along the curve of her navel.

I lifted her up, cradling her ass, and she wrapped her legs even more tightly around me as I carried her the three steps to the bed. I laid her back on the bed and she stretched out, giving me a sexy look that I couldn't fucking get enough of, loose dark hairs from her ponytail falling in her eyes. Goddamn, if this wasn't every man's wet dream, I didn't know what was.

I ripped off my shirt, lowered my jeans to the ground, then climbed on the bed, hovering over her. She helped to pull the dress over her head, and I slipped the tie from the back of her head so her dark hair spilled over her shoulders.

"I want you to fuck me hard. . ." She commanded, licking her lips, picking up the band of my boxer briefs, and dipping her hand inside. She curled her fingers around my cock, stroking it slowly. "But first, I want to taste your cock."

I couldn't possibly say no to that.

She bit her lip as I nudged my boxer briefs down to my knees. She knelt on the side of me, still playing with my balls. "I love your cock, Zain."

She lifted the weight of my cock, feeling it in her hand, and leaned forward. She touched her tongue to the very tip, which was enough to tear a groan of pleasure from my throat. Her tongue a white-hot, electric spear, flicked just over the top at first, then trailed downward, over the mushroom tip.

She licked on, traveling down the length of me, until I let out a tortured moan and my head fell back against the pillow. Her mouth was so hot, so wet, so perfect. I gazed at the ceiling, then closed my eyes. I had wanted to watch her first explorations, but this was on its way to being the best damn blowjob I'd ever received.

I threaded my fingers through her hair and groaned as she took the whole head into her mouth, surrounding me fully. She flicked her tongue over the surface in quick, circular motions. I was hard as a rock by then.

Suddenly, she opened her mouth and sucked down, far, far, far, until I scraped the back of her throat.

"God, that's phenomenal. Just like that," I murmured, pushing her head back down when she came up.

But I didn't need to show her anything. She had this. She knew just what she needed to do to drive me wild. She sucked me in deeper still, the next time, and again, until my cock was pulsating and begging for release.

"Come here," I said, motioning her up to me.

She slinked up to me, hovering over my body so that her tits hung down, nipples grazing my chest. I took one of them in my hand, running a finger over the nipple.

"You're so gorgeous," I said, my cock hard between us. I kissed her cheek, took her earlobe into my mouth, sucking on it. "I have to be inside you."

"Oh. Please, Zain."

"All right." Taking a breath, I lifted her carefully, positioning her back on the mattress, and rolled those little panties off of her hips. I climbed over her, positioning myself between her legs, resting on one forearm as I kissed her deeply. I settled myself at the entrance, just inches from euphoria.

"I can't wait any longer." I thrust in, hard, dragging all the air out of both of our lungs.

I lowered my mouth against hers and kissed her, hot and urgent. Her hand trailed down the curve of my back, cupping my ass. "Fuck me. Please. Zain—"

I slowly pulled out in a slick, frictionless slide. My cock leaving her, coming out halfway, made an emptiness that was almost physical pain. Her delicate hand gently nudged my ass back, and I couldn't contain my excitement. I suddenly thrust into her, forcing a moan out of her throat.

"Oh," she moaned. "Oh, fuck."

I loved it when she talked dirty like that, a sound that only made me want to keep this going, keep fucking her forever. My next thrust made her pussy clench in pleasure, and the next time, she rocked in rhythm with me, meeting each thrust with her own.

Hips to hips, heart against heart, tongues working in chorus, until we were only one being, two halves of a whole, working in perfect synchronicity. The buzzing in my body built to a world-shattering crescendo.

Suddenly, I felt her tense in my arms, and she let out another moan. "Oh God, I'm coming."

I thrust into her, grinding, again and again, moaning more as I kissed her, stopping and stuttering, losing the rhythm, finding it again, until I went screaming over the edge.

She held me close, so tight then, sinking her teeth into my shoulder. "Oh, Zain," she said, whispering my name as I exploded into her. My mouth went to her throat, sucking on it, devouring her down to her tits as I came deep inside her.

We lay there for a while, panting, as I rested my forehead on her shoulder. Then I slowly slid out and crawled next to her.

"I love you," she whispered as she wrapped her arms around me.

And then I did a total dick thing, the only thing I could think of to do. I nodded at her, speechless. Because I'd fucked hundreds of women before and never felt a single thing afterward. Especially love.

But this? This was uncharted territory for me.

I didn't know what it was, but it wasn't *nothing*. It could've been love. So I took a deep breath, kissed her forehead, and said, "I'll never let anything happen to you. I won't let Viktor, or anyone else who threatens you near you, you understand?"

"Anyone else?" she asked. "Like who?"

"Just . . . anyone."

That seemed to be all she wanted to hear. She settled against me, her breathing slowing. I waited for her to tell me it was time to leave, because she didn't want me getting too comfortable, but she never did. We were in danger of falling asleep and blowing her rules all to hell.

A few moments later, when I had almost dozed off, and I was pretty sure she had, too, I heard the familiar buzzing of my phone. Sasha let out a little murmur and yawned but didn't wake up as I slipped out from under her head, replacing my shoulder with a pillow.

I found my boxer briefs in the pile of discarded clothes and slid them on. I found my phone just where I'd left it, in the pocket of my jeans.

My phone had been buzzing steadily since I'd left the clubhouse. Now, for the first time, I opened it up and saw I had dozens of messages, from all of my brothers. They were shitting bricks over me leaving.

The call coming through, though, was from Cullen. Looking over at Sasha's sleeping form, the pretty, graceful curve of her spine, I slipped out to the living room and answered.

"Yeah?"

"Listen," Cullen said, his voice gruff. "You need to come back."

I laughed. "Is that you talking or did the other guys put you up to it?"

"It's me. Look, we can figure this out. But what's not going to work is you walking out on us every time the going gets tough. So come back to the clubhouse and let's talk this shit out."

I frowned. "I'm telling you, Cullen. You can talk all you want to me. But it's not going to work if you insist on working with that motherfucker."

"All right. I get it. I get you hate him and can't work with him. But we can figure it out. Just . . . get over here. Okay?"

I looked down the hallway, toward the bedrooms, and sighed. I had to leave Sasha's place, anyway. And what would I do, otherwise? Go home and contemplate my meaningless life of not being part of a club for the first time in years?

Yeah, no. That would be sheer misery. I was glad Cullen was open to talking about it. He was not only a great president, but a great guy. I just wasn't too sure I was going to like the terms. "All right. I'll be there in ten."

I hung up the phone and went to the bedroom, where I pulled on the rest of my clothes. As I did, Sasha rolled over in bed, a sleepy smile on her face. "You've got to leave?"

I nodded. She looked so damn fuckable as usual, and my cock twitched again.

But I had things to do.

"Thought you wanted me to?" I asked.

She laughed. "Maybe not this soon."

I kissed her forehead. If only I could stay. But I knew I'd be back. Sooner, rather than later. My body was already craving her again. "I'll call you."

She settled against the pillow and closed her eyes, so I went to the front door, locked it, and closed it behind me, making sure no one could get in. There was no telling what threats lurked around these areas for a Cobras girl, and I wanted to deliver on my promise to keep her and Alena as safe as possible.

Chapter Twenty-Four

Sasha

I rolled over in bed, feeling so thoroughly and deliciously fucked that I probably could've flown.

And already, I wanted more.

Was it normal for a grown woman to feel so much like a kid in a candy store? I couldn't control my urges where this man was concerned.

Then I felt the side of the bed and remembered Zain kissing me goodbye and leaving.

I sighed, grabbing his pillow and bringing it to my face. It still smelled a little like him, the spicy masculine scent of motorcycles and man that made my insides tingle.

The pillow wasn't a good enough substitute for the man, though. Obviously.

I lay there, watching the curtains move in the breeze, as moonlight filtered in through my window, and thought of what he'd said. Something about keeping me safe from Viktor or anyone else.

Who else?

Was there someone else I was supposed to be worrying about? I hadn't thought anyone could be worse than Viktor. But then again, Viktor wouldn't touch me, and he'd kill himself before ever he hurt Alena. As insane as he drove me, I knew that to my core.

And these people that Viktor was helping Zain to get rid of?

I knew nothing about them. Except that Zain and his men had called in reinforcements like my ex to help get rid of them.

I thought of the man on the motorcycle that was watching us yesterday morning. I should've told Zain about him. What if he was part of the other club? What if just by associating with Zain, I'd made myself a target?

I should have asked him about that. Because maybe he wasn't as concerned about Viktor as he was about protecting me from these other people.

A chill skittered down my spine. Now I was wide-awake. No hope for sleep.

As I climbed out of bed, a fierce wind whistled through the window, sending the curtains blowing. The weather was changing. I parted the curtains and closed the window so it was only open a couple of inches, then found some boxers and a camisole to change into.

I pushed open the door and went down to Alena's room. In the dim pink glow of her nightlight, I could see the profile of her angelic face as she hugged one of her stuffed princess dolls. The window in her room was also open, the wind blowing the curtains steadily, so I went and closed it a couple inches, too. Bending over to kiss her little forehead, I walked out to the hall to make sure the door was locked.

Of course, it was. Zain wanted us safe, so he wouldn't leave it open as an invitation to criminals.

I looked around, shivering as I thought of the ways he'd kissed me, touched me, right on that very spot.

I'd told him I loved him.

Maybe I should've been cringing at that, but I didn't. It was true. Sure, I'd only loved one other man before him and look how that had turned out. But all I needed to do was look at Zain and I knew things would be different.

He was different.

Okay, it was probably too early to be professing my love for him. After all, I'd just met him. But I'd been raised to believe that love was something precious and hard to find, and when it was found, it shouldn't be treated as an afterthought.

And I had it right, this time. I just knew it.

The only thing was, I wasn't really sure he was the type who'd settle down. There was not a single thing about Zain that said to me he wanted the kids and the white picket fence. And yes, he'd told me he'd take care of me. But maybe he meant for *now* not *forever*.

I needed a forever. Stability. I'd rather have to do it alone than have men coming in and out of Alena's life.

I went to the kitchen and got myself a bottle of water, deciding that the next time I talked to Zain, damn his sexiness . . . I'd be firm. I wouldn't crumple into his arms and beg him to fuck me. Next time, I'd tell him that if he didn't want this—us—for keeps, I wasn't interested.

As I was sucking down a gulp of water, I heard a crashing sound coming from down the hallway.

I dropped the water on the counter and ran for it, peering in my room. At first I thought the wind had managed to knock something off my nightstand.

But there was nothing on the ground, and the curtains in my window weren't blowing at all.

That was odd.

My blood started to pound inside my ears as it hit me. Alena.

Backing out of my room, I raced down the hall and burst into Alena's room.

The first thing my eyes fell upon was her princess lamp, the base shattered, on the ground. Then, the wide-open window.

And then, the empty bed, with the covers pulled back.

I raced for the window and peered out past the shredded screen. But I saw nothing but darkness and heard nothing but the whistling of the wind and the sound of my own heart, slamming against my chest.

Chapter Twenty-Five

Zain

When I cruised down the pier and pulled up at the clubhouse, Cullen was sitting on an old picnic table right outside the front door. He was smoking a cigarette, which wasn't like him. We all knew he'd been trying to quit, because of his little daughter, Ella. Until now, I'd thought he had succeeded.

He breathed out a long cloud of smoke as I approached him. "So . . . this girl of yours."

"Sasha," I mumbled.

"Yeah. Her. You get with her out of spite for Viktor? Is that what it is?"

"Hell, no. I met her before I met Viktor," I said, leaning against the picnic table and taking the cigarette and lighter he offered me.

I sucked in the raw taste of the tobacco, trying to get it to calm me.

"And she means something to you?"

I let out a low chuckle. He had to ask, after I nearly gave up the Cobras on her account. "What the fuck do you think?"

He scratched the side of his face and looked out over the black line of ocean in the darkness. "I think it's a big problem." He took another drag. "And I also know you go through women like nobody's business."

"And you didn't, before Grace?" I snapped back, getting annoyed. "Did you call me here to fuck with me, or are we going to figure this out, man?"

He hitched a shoulder. "I just want you to know that whatever we come up with here, it ain't gonna be easy from here on out. So you need to make sure she's worth it."

"Jesus, Cullen. If I was willing to walk out on the club, that should show you. I'm not fucking around," I muttered.

"Yeah, about that—"

Here it comes, I thought. Where walking out on the Fury meant certain death, walking out on the Cobras simply wasn't done. I think when I said that to Cullen, his mind probably exploded.

"Look," I said, stopping him in his tracks. "I know you and my brothers. I know you guys have always stood up for what is right. Which is what attracted me to you in the first place. But you turning a blind eye to an asshole who abused his wife? That ain't like us. And working with him? That doesn't sit well with me. Forget about how I feel about Sasha. The Cobras should not be in bed with an asshole like that, and you know it."

He thought about that for a minute, then flicked the butt of his cigarette onto the pavement. "Yeah. Probably not. Only problem is, and I hate to even say it, but I don't know what else to do. The Hell's Fury is breathing down our neck, and I want to get rid of them once and for all. We can with Viktor's help. Then we go back to normal working with Moscow. If not, we're toast."

Right. I knew. We lose our client, we don't operate anymore, and the Fury spreads all over Aveline Bay, then the whole West Coast.

"I get it. But I'd rather fucking die fighting the Fury than hop into bed with that fucker," I said flatly.

"You might be okay with that. But I'm not willing to lose a bunch of Cobra lives. That'll be on my conscience." He pushed off the picnic bench and said, "So how can I change your mind?"

I nearly laughed out loud. He was serious? "You didn't get it from what I just said? You can't. I'm not fucking working with that guy."

"I get what you're saying. You think he's an asshole. You don't want to be on his side. But what if we're not on his side?"

I squinted at him. "I don't follow."

"Look. You don't have to like the kind of toilet paper that's on the roll. You just use it, because it gets the job done. So we use Viktor the same way? Don't agree with him, fine. Think he's an asshole, great. But let's use him to get the job done, and then we can wipe our hands of him forever. You understand?"

I shook my head.

"Look man. I never said that our relationship with Viktor is forever. Once this is over, he can crawl back into the shithole he came from, and I won't care. But what I do care about is my brothers. We are forever. You get that? And he may be an asshole, but I'm happy to use him to make sure that none of my brothers, the people I really care about, get killed."

I laced my hands in front of me and stared down at the rotting wood plank between my feet. It was dark, but in the moonlight, the little flecks of glass in the asphalt glistened.

"All right. Fine. But what difference does it make? Even if I did agree to this, Viktor's gone. He'd probably already told—"

"He's inside," he said, motioning to the door.

I looked around. Sure enough, I spotted the nondescript black sedan he drove, parked in the row, among the other cars. I let out a sour laugh. "And I suppose you want me to talk to him and make nice."

He shrugged. "You don't got to make nice. You just got to not want to kill each other. Think you can do that?"

"Well—"

"So that means not fucking telling him about how good a fuck his ex-wife is. Understand?"

I supposed. Although, a little sadistic part of me wanted to do that. I knew Cullen was right, though. I didn't have to like him, but he was a solution. For now. And Sasha was right, also. Asshole that he was, he was still Alena's dad.

I gritted my teeth and pushed up off the picnic bench, the splinters catching in the seat of my jeans. "Fine. Lead the way."

We walked inside, me bringing up the rear. The second we got inside and the door slammed behind me, Viktor flew off his chair and charged me, screaming a bunch of shit in Russian.

I crossed my arms, not wanting to get into it, since I'd promised Cullen, but prepared to stand my ground and protect myself if I had to. The whole, I fucked your wife taunt was pretty heavy in my head right then as he shouted in my face, spittle flying. Instead, I just smirked at him.

"Whoa, whoa, whoa," Cullen said, stepping between us. "We're here to just talk."

"You didn't tell me he'd be back. I thought you got rid of him," Viktor grumbled, giving Cullen a sidelong glance. "I came back against my better judgment. I should call the men in Moscow and tell them the deal is off."

"Look. First thing. We don't have to like each other," I said, keeping my voice calm. "But it's in all our best interest to take the Fury out. You know that. We need them gone so we can continue to conduct our business in peace. And I know your contacts are paying you handsomely to do that. So let's just get it done. Deal?"

I reached my hand out to shake his.

He stared at it for a while, like it was crawling with ants. Then, reluctantly, he shook it.

As he did, I grabbed his thick, sweaty hand, yanking it back and wrenching it behind his back. He let out a growl as I pushed him face first up against the wall. He and Cullen let out a "What the fuck—" at the same time, but I ignored it.

"Second thing," I growled into his ear. "Sasha is not your property, comrade. She's not yours anymore, so don't fuck with her. She's allowed to see who she wants. You get it?"

His face turned red, and the vein on his head bulged purple as his cheek pressed up against the cold cement wall. "You fucking—"

I wrenched his arm back harder, so something popped. He let out a growl.

"What did you say?"

"Fine. I don't control Sasha."

Slowly, I let him go, and backed away to see Cullen, staring at me with a look that said, *you fucking asshole. Couldn't help yourself, could you?*

I smiled at him. "Good. Don't forget it."

Viktor peeled himself away from the wall, turned, and adjusted his blazer over his boxy form. His face was losing the red color, but it was still pink. His eyes were hard on me. "You asshole," he said, lunging for me again.

I tightened my hands into fists, ready to answer.

I didn't get a chance to. The second he got within striking distance, the door swung open and a face, as white as the moon, appeared in the door.

All eyes in the place swung toward it.

It was Sasha, shaking like crazy, her eyes wide with worry. I didn't have time to ask how she'd found us, because it was obvious something was wrong.

"What is it?" Viktor and I both said at once.

"Alena," she whispered, breathless. "She's gone. Someone came in her window and took her from her bed."

Chapter Twenty-Six

Sasha

I wasn't thinking clearly on the ride to the clubhouse.

I was thinking of Alena. She'd only ever been with either me or Viktor. She had to have been frightened out of her mind, wherever she was. She was only four. My mind kept flipping through hundreds of awful scenarios as I sped through the streets on the way to the pier.

All I knew was that was where I'd seen Viktor and Zain, all those weeks ago, and something told me that that was where at least one of them would be.

I didn't expect to find them both. Predictably, they were both frowning, shaking, on the verge of killing each other.

But they stopped when I came in. Breathless, shaking, I told them that Alena was missing, and suddenly, the tension in the place shifted.

Zain's face darkened as he turned to the other man standing next to him. "Fury," he murmured.

Viktor punched the air with a fist. "Fuck!"

My breath hitched. "What? What does this mean? Do you mean that the other club has her?"

Zain shook his head and gritted his teeth before his said, "Fuck! I was afraid this would happen."

I shouted at him "You were? Then why didn't you tell me?" I ran to punch him, hit him, but he took my wrists and pulled me to him. Instead of hitting him, I wound up sobbing into his t-shirt. He wrapped his arms around me and smoothed my hair as I cried.

"Fuck the element of surprise. They must know about Viktor," the other man said.

Zain shook his head. "No. They just know I was with Sasha. They're trying to get even with me."

ZAIN

When I managed to open my eyes, I saw Viktor, staring at me with his top lip raised in a snarl. "Sasha!" he barked.

I slipped away from Zain's body and wiped at my eyes. I wanted to say something calming to my ex-husband, but from the look on his face, I knew that was impossible. He was so angry. I reached for him, but before I could say a word, he wheeled on Zain.

"This is all your fault, *mudak*," he growled out, coming between Zain and me. "You think playing around with my wife wouldn't end up hurting anyone? Now my daughter is in the hands of those bastards and it's because of you putting your dick where it didn't belong. After I kill these motherfuckers, you're next. I'll have your head on a platter!"

I was used to being quiet and falling in line with Viktor. But for the first time, something inside me overflowed, and I threw myself in front of him, shoving him hard.

"No!" I shouted, finding my voice, tears spilling from my eyes as I pushed Viktor away. "You will not!

345

Don't you see? You're just as dangerous. A killer? For all these years, you put Alena in as much danger as he did!"

He stared at me in silent shock.

I swiped the back of my hand across my face, wiping away the tears. "Besides, this time, it's my fault, Viktor. I did this because I took my eyes off her. But it doesn't matter. What matters is that Alena's gone, and we need to get her back. Please. Let's just focus on getting her back."

Viktor's cold eyes fell on me, and for a moment I thought he might pull out a gun and finish Zain right there. Funny, when I first met Viktor, I didn't see him as a killer, but now, looking at him, his face contorted in rage, I couldn't see him as anything else.

Then he said, "Yes. We must get her back at all costs."

"And the only way to do that is if we work together," I told him. "You need to work with Zain. Stop fighting him and put aside your differences, for just this once."

Viktor's face contorted in a snarl. Then he gave Zain an almost imperceptible nod. "All right."

Zain accepted his word and spoke to the other man. "Cullen, we need to get all the men here. Now. We get Alena back tonight, and we put an end to the Fury for good. Tonight."

"Yeah," the man called Cullen said, fishing his phone out of the pocket of his jeans. From the way they were all looking at him, I could tell he must be an important man in the group. "Let's do this."

EVIE MONROE

Chapter Twenty-Seven

Zain

Sasha was a hot mess. I couldn't blame her. But I knew what the Fury was capable of. She had no idea. If she knew, she'd probably have been a hell of a lot worse. So I tried to keep her occupied while we waited for the rest of the guys. We talked low about inconsequential things. She asked me how I got each of my tattoos, so I told her.

"This one, I got before I became a Cobra," I said, pointing to the tattoo on my left bicep. I dipped down my t-shirt and pointed to the one on my right shoulder. "This was the first one I got, when I was eighteen. I was a stupid shit and thought skulls were cool and made me look tough."

She tilted her head. "You look tough."

"Not then. I was about a hundred pounds, soaking wet. But I thought I was pretty cool. No one could tell me shit."

She nodded. "I was the same way when I was eighteen. Isn't everyone?"

"Yeah, but I was the worst at it." I pointed at my neck. "I got this one a few years ago."

"It looks like a snake, too," she said, tracing her finger over it. "A snake eating itself."

I nodded. "It's a Greek *Ouroboros*. A serpent eating its own end is a symbol for rebirth, remaking ourselves. When my parents died, I decided who I wanted to be. I decided I had the power to change myself and make myself who I wanted."

She smiled, stroking it, as I looked over at Viktor. He had his upper lip curled in a snarl, watching his ex-wife touch me.

Maybe I shouldn't have taunted him that way. But while he was focused on that, I was focused on taking care of Sasha. Fuck him for not being secure enough in his manhood to let her do what she wanted. That was his problem, and he was paying for it now. Right now, I needed to calm Sasha down. If I had to put my tongue down her throat in front of him to do it, I'd do it.

The rest of the men arrived quickly. When we all were assembled around the table, I introduced Sasha to my brothers and said, "The Fury have her daughter. Viktor's daughter. Her name's Alena."

She lifted her phone and showed them all a picture of the little girl, hair in pigtails, looking just about as heartbreakingly cute as a kid could be. "She's only four."

Around the table, frowns deepened. Nix shot his hands in the air and cursed. "So we're doing this? Now?"

Cullen nodded. "Yeah. Get into the back and load up some arms. We're going to hit them hard. No mercy this time."

Viktor added, "Waste no time. We've got to get to them."

"But we have to make sure Alena is safe, first," Sasha put in, standing up. "Please."

I jumped up and wrapped an arm around her. "That's right. The girl's safety is our top priority. Whatever we have to do to get her back, we do."

Cullen clapped his hands together and pointed to the door. "All right. Viktor's intel says they're at their clubhouse near Sunset. Let's meet at the Circle K there. We'll head in together. Got it?"

Everyone started to head out. Sasha hugged herself, looking up at me. Viktor should've been at the head of the charge, but instead, he hung back, watching her.

"Sasha," he called to her.

She looked at him. "Get our daughter back, Viktor."

He nodded, gave me eye-daggers, and headed out the door. She shook her head and sighed. "Please don't let whatever differences you have get in the way of saving Alena. Promise me that."

I pulled her to me and touched her cheek gently. "I promise. You stay here. Try not to worry. I'll make sure she's safe. I'll text you as soon as I have her."

Tears flooded her eyes. "Thank you."

Stooping down, I kissed her forehead. She nudged me to the door. "Hurry."

Outside, the men were already on their bikes, heading out toward our rendezvous point. Viktor was already gone. I jumped on my bike and followed after them, hoping that I could keep that promise and that Alena would be safe. I thought about Joel. How we'd tried to keep him safe. Alive.

My stomach churned. She was just a baby girl.

I was ready to fight the fucking Fury, to kill them. Every single Cobra had their own war to fight with the Fury, and each one of us felt the same way. Tonight, we'd each get our long-awaited vengeance.

We rallied at the Circle K and decided to roll up on them using a minimal number of bikes so that they wouldn't hear us coming. Their club was an old warehouse in a rough section of town, the same place where Joel had met his end. We knew the area well. The police wouldn't come for a few gunshots unless it turned into a bloodbath. We'd be gone by then. We also knew plenty of ways in and out of the abandoned building, once we got beyond the chain-link fence.

The street was dark when we got there. Just a couple of dim streetlights around the burned out shells of buildings, all of them open and dark.

We parked in a narrow alley, grabbed whatever weapons we could hold, and headed out to the side of the building they used as their clubhouse, staying behind the fence. We spotted at least twenty Fury men outside, hanging around a giant fire in an oil drum, drinking, laughing, having a great time despite the fact that a kid had died there, a hundred yards away just a few weeks ago.

"Remember guys," Cullen whispered. "Keep our presence on the DL as long as possible. We need to find the girl, and the sooner they find out we're here, the worse it'll be for her."

Cullen motioned for us to split up and go different ways around the building. Somehow, I ended up with Viktor and Hart, having to creep around the weeds in the front of the building.

Crouching low to the ground, I took the lead, keeping my hand on my piece. Viktor followed behind. "We should take them out from here. Through the fence."

"Not from here," I murmured low. "We start firing, they'll be on us like flies on shit."

We got up to the fence, and I peered around to have a look. I could hear a couple of men talking right inside, just a couple yards away.. They faced away from us, prime material for a sneak attack. I motioned to Viktor and Hart to keep quiet, put our guns away, and subdue them with our fists, which would help us stay as undetected as possible.

On three, we jumped the men, each of us taking one. We dragged them into the alley and shot them with relative ease. The silencers worked.

We crossed to the other side of the fence where a few more guys were hanging toward the edge of the gathering. This time, Viktor motioned, and I nodded.

We managed to take out six more guys, as fast and quietly as possible. By that time, I was feeling an uneasy kind of compromise with Viktor, like we were working as part of a team. With the body count piling up, we were able to get into the courtyard and sneak into one of the entrances.

Once inside, we crouched down in a stairwell that led both up and down, listening for sounds. We heard someone moving around and strains of music coming from upstairs. Viktor motioned up that way with his chin, and I nodded and slid up the stairs.

I poked my head out the door on the second floor and noticed a light coming from under one of the doors. An old manufacturing building, the second floor was strewn with garbage and looked like the old offices for management. The three of us crept down the hallway, toward the light. I pressed up against the wall outside the door and listened.

"Scar says they ain't gonna try nothing tonight," a guy said. "They ain't stupid. We got the numbers on them."

The other guy said something back that I couldn't make out.

Then the man started to walk out, and I realized he was just a kid. Maybe sixteen—eighteen? He got part of the way down the hallway when Viktor grabbed him from behind and held a gun up to his head.

I grinned at him. "Guess we are stupid, motherfucker," I mumbled, making sure the other guy hadn't come out, too. "Take us to the girl."

"What girl?" he said, his voice strangled by Viktor's big arm braced around his neck.

I made the motion like I was going to knee him in the balls. "Don't give me that shit unless you want a broken neck."

He swallowed. "Okay. Okay. I'll take you there."

He led the way down the dark hallway to a room in the back of the warehouse, stumbling every so often.

Every time he did, Viktor kicked him. When the door was in view, the first thing we saw were two men standing outside. They leveled their guns at us.

Before I could react, Viktor fired off two rounds, hitting each one squarely in the chest.

He was a damn good shot.

Then, as if in slow motion, all hell broke loose.

People yelled and came running. The kid who'd led us to the room took one look at his dead friends and wheeled on us, trying to fight, so I put a bullet in his head. Some guys appeared in the hallway, but Hart started shooting, motioning at me to go forward. "I got this. Go get the girl."

Viktor and I lunged forward toward the room the men had been guarding.

Before we got there, I heard her. A little girl's hysterical sobs.

I tried the door. Locked. I shot at the doorknob, splintering the wood and pushed the door open.

Alena was sitting there, on an old mattress, in her nightgown. Her cheeks were red and wet with tears. I bridged the distance in a single step and scooped her up. "You okay Alena? They hurt you?"

She shook her head and looked behind me. "Daddy?" she asked, hardly able to believe the two of us showed up together. "Daddy!"

She reached out her arms to him, and he snapped her up. She wrapped her arms and legs tightly around the big man. The look he gave me surprised the hell out of me. I think it was gratitude.

"Go!" I said to him. "I'll cover you."

We headed out to the front, down the stairs, and out the door we'd come in. As we got to the courtyard, more gunshots rang out. I felt them close, whizzing by my ears, the bullets burying themselves in the brick façade of the old building behind us.

"Keep running!" I shouted at Viktor, who never stopped. I got behind the wall and started to shoot, blindly, not sure who the hell I was up against.

I got off a few more shots, stopped to reload, and when I looked again, Alena and Viktor were gone. They'd escaped from the courtyard.

Good.

But the shooting just kept going on, into the night. And I was more than ready to give every one of these Fury motherfuckers their due. Once and for all.

Chapter Twenty-Eight

Sasha

I'd had some pretty terrible nights before. Nights when Viktor was gone, and I was alone with Alena. I had no escape and wondered if I'd ever have a life that Viktor didn't control for me.

But I never thought there'd ever be a night as long as this one.

I sat on the sofa at the clubhouse with some inane reality show on television. I couldn't focus on it, instead, I twisted the locket around my neck that Alena had given me as a Mother's Day present last year. It was the one that had a tiny baby picture of her inside, taken in the hospital when she was small and wrinkled. I could still remember peering into the bassinette at the hospital and thinking that my life was changed forever, and in a good way.

Tonight, I had that same feeling. But I couldn't tell which way things would go—good or bad. I trusted Zain and knew Viktor would do everything possible to save Alena, but some things were out of even their control. I think that was what scared me the most.

All I kept thinking was that it didn't matter whose fault it was. I was her mom, and it was my duty to look after her. If anything happened to Alena, I'd never forgive myself.

And of course, I worried about them. Not just Zain, but Viktor, too. Finally, I understood why he'd kept his business from me. Kept me so sheltered. Not just because he wanted me safe; he wanted to spare me the stress of it all.

So was it silly for me to fall into more of that danger with Zain? Maybe involving myself with a motorcycle club and being Zain's girlfriend? Would I always be worrying about him, as long as we were together? Would I learn to depend on him and fall for him only to have him taken from me?

Oh, well, Sasha. Too late. You know you've already fallen for him, a little voice in my head said.

That was true. I was in love with Zain. And that scared me.

As I waited at the club, the door opened and a young woman with strawberry blonde hair appeared, holding a sleeping child in her arms. "Hi!" she greeted me. "Are you Sasha?"

I nodded, confused as she came up close to me and laid the sleeping kid down on the sofa beside me. I stood up to give her more room as she said, "I'm Grace. Cullen's girlfriend." she said with a smile. "You know, he's the president here."

"Oh," I said, too shocked to say more. So he had a girlfriend.

"Yeah, Cullen called me and told me what happened. I'm so sorry. I thought if it was Ella here, I'd be freaking out," she said, motioning to her daughter and covering her with a blanket.

I switched off the television set, and we moved to the other side of the clubhouse to let the girl sleep.

"So I decided to keep you company. You don't mind?"

I smiled. She was so sweet. It was hard to believe that big, tough ball of testosterone and tattoos had such a nice and pretty other half. "That's so nice. And yes, I'm going crazy with worry."

She nodded, her face so full of sympathy, one would think her own child had been kidnapped. Then she wrapped her arms around me in a big, comforting hug. I slumped against her, wanting to cry. It was exactly what I needed at that moment.

"Hell's Fury are awful," she said when she let go. "They'll get their due. The men will make sure of it. I have no doubt. And they'll get your daughter back. I'm sure of it."

The confidence in her voice made me feel a lot better.

We sat down at the table at the front of the clubhouse. "Good. Anyway, the other girls'll be here soon."

"Other girls?"

What happened next surprised me. Over the next half-hour, a number of women arrived at the clubhouse, turning the place into a party. There was a willowy blonde named Liv, whose pregnant belly was so big, I thought she might give birth at any moment. She introduced herself as Nix's girlfriend. Then there was a pretty redhead named Cait, Drake's girlfriend, and Roxanne, her mom. Next, a girl with dark brown hair and eyes named Charlotte, who was Hart's girlfriend. And last, a woman with a dark ponytail, named Nora, who was Jet's girlfriend.

There were so many of them!

Each time one of them arrived, Grace would give her a big smile and say, "Oh look! Hi, so-and-so!" and then she would whisper a little bit about whoever it was, before giving each of them a warm hug. When Nora arrived, she whispered, "She's the most brilliant surgeon. If any of our people are hurt, she'll take care of them."

"Oh," I whispered, impressed, feeling better yet.

They all seemed to know each other and gave each other hugs. After Grace introduced each woman to me, it was the same. They would all express their sympathy and give me a hug, too, like I'd already been inducted into their group. The family.

Before long, it was a regular party. Some of them had brought things to eat, and one of the women had brought a few bottles of wine. I wasn't hungry, but I did have a glass of wine to calm my nerves. As they all chatted, it was clear to me they'd been through things like this before, and they often got together when their men were out fighting.

Maybe it was that I hadn't seen my family in so long—or because they'd been rather distant? But instantly, I felt like I was home. It made my heart hurt, how much I wanted to be a part of what these women had.

They all must've seen how nervous I was, because they kept saying reassuring things to me. Nora put a hand over mine. "Don't worry. They look out for one another. They've been through some pretty rough times."

Grace drained her glass of wine and nodded. "And Cullen says it ends tonight. I trust him when he says that. He's a man of his word."

"I can't stop thinking of Alena. She must be so afraid," I said, my heart clenching at the thought. "Alena is my life. And I feel like I am the one who put her in danger."

Across the way, Liv, with both hands on her pregnant belly, shook her head. "Oh, no, it's not your fault!"

Cait leaned over and hugged me from behind. "Don't beat yourself up, Sasha. Really. It isn't. And you'll see. Our men will get her home safe. We'll all get through this. Together."

The stabbing pain in my chest slowly subsided, and I smiled and took another drink from my glass. The girls started talking about other things, inconsequential things like the weather and new television shows they'd been bingeing on, and I tried to keep up with the conversation, but every few seconds, my mind would drift back to Alena.

A moment later, I heard a car pull up outside the warehouse. I jumped up just as the door flung open, and Viktor stormed in, carrying Alena in his arms.

I gasped, as did all of my new friends.

As he stalked across the room to me, I inspected her. She looked alert, swinging her head back and forth in effort to catch a glimpse of me. When she saw me, she shouted in glee, "Mommy!"

"Alena!" I cried as Viktor deposited her in my arms. I was still doing the visual inspection. Two arms, two legs, no visible bruises or cuts anywhere. The worst thing was her crazy bedhead. "Are you okay?"

"Yes, I am, Mommy," she said, resting her head on my shoulder. "Some mean men took me out of bed while I was sleeping. They were stinky."

I looked over at Viktor, who was standing there. Before I could say anything, Grace asked, "What's happening over there?"

He spoke, low and grave. "I don't know. I needed to get Alena out of there as soon as possible. Lots of gunshots as I was leaving."

"Are you all right?" I asked.

"Yes. Fine."

I swallowed. "Zain?"

His mouth puckered into a snarl. "I left him there."

I didn't ask more. It was clear he didn't want to talk about him. Maybe he didn't know. Maybe I didn't want to know.

I hugged Alena to my chest, imagining the worst.

EVIE MONROE

Chapter Twenty-Nine

Zain

So it turned out, even though I'd been the one to start everything with the Fury, I was the one to end it, too. And that felt good.

I fired my gun, and the last guy fell. To my delight, it was Scar, their new President.

I paused to reload again and looked up. Blood surging through my veins, I looked around for my next victim.

But everything was silent. Cobras stood all around me, surveying the damage.

The Fury clubhouse looked a lot like a morgue by the time we got done with them. Hart and I were the last to leave. We combed the place, looking for the others, and found that the place was empty. Stepping over bodies, I shook my head, then listened, but heard nothing. "We got them all?"

Hart nodded. "The ones we didn't get must have ran away. Fucking pussies."

"Holy shit." I couldn't believe that the six of us, plus Viktor and two of his guys wreaked this much havoc on the Fury. I knew we were out for blood, but I never imagined it like this.

I thought I'd feel a lot worse about killing people, but I felt no guilt. Just damn good. Glad that those assholes had finally gotten what was coming to them. They'd had chance after chance to turn it around and leave us alone, and they'd pushed us too far. They'd deserved no mercy.

Especially after what they'd done to that poor kid, Joel.

But Viktor had been right. He'd known exactly when and where to come after them, and now, we were done with the Fury. We could live in peace.

Hart and I hopped on his bike and took it back to our rendezvous point. There, we saw Drake tending to Jet for a gunshot wound to the shoulder. Cullen and

Nix were there, too, giving each other fist-bumps. Other than a few close calls and some bruises, we were okay.

"Why didn't we do that sooner?" Jet said with a grin when we arrived. "They're done. Jesus, I feel good."

Adrenaline pumping in our veins, the rest of us joined in when he let out a loud whoop, until the owner of the gas station came out and glared at us. Cullen waved at him and told us all to meet up at the clubhouse. "I just texted Grace to let her know we're on our way."

Drake punched Jet, who'd bled through his white t-shirt. "Yeah, I'm sure you'd rather have your girl sew you up this time," he said.

He laughed. "She sure as fuck has better bedside manner than you do."

We all hopped back on our bikes and went back to the clubhouse, to continue the party. When we got there, the girls were all there, already celebrating the news.

When I went inside, Sasha rushed up to me and wrapped her arms around me, hugging me tight. "I really thought I might never see you again," she breathed out.

"Shh," I said, smoothing her hair. "I told you everything would be okay."

"When Viktor came back with Alena, I was worried something had happened to you."

"No. Just cleaning up and finishing the job. We decimated the Fury."

She inhaled sharply against me but didn't say anything.

"I wanted Alena to come home to you first because I knew you would be worried about her."

"I was worried about *both* of you," she pointed out.

"Aw, baby, you don't have to," I said, kissing the top of her head. "But I'm glad you do. I love you, too. How's Alena?"

She pulled back, a shocked look on her face. "You . . . do?"

I laughed. "I told you I did, didn't I?"

She shook her head.

"Oh, Right. I told you that you meant more to me than the club. And you should know by now how much I love my club."

She gave me a sheepish expression. "I see why you love the club. I shouldn't have made you have to decide between the two of us."

I stroked her cheek. "All right. Club rules are the club always comes first. But for me," I leaned down and whispered in her ear, "you always come first. If you ever want me to—"

"No. I won't."

I squeezed her hand. She seemed so resolute. I had to wonder just what the girls had said to her, to make her so sure. Maybe it was just knowing that she wasn't the only girl of an MC guy. Maybe it was that the Fury were now gone. Maybe it was that she realized, just like I had, that she and I belonged together. "How's Alena?" I repeated.

She smiled. "Fine. She's sleeping on the sofa, next to Ella. She was so tired, obviously. But thanks to you, she seems fine. Like her old self."

I shrugged. "It wasn't just me. It was all of us. Even—" I looked around and saw the devil I was about to speak about, stalking up to us. He looked pissed, like now that he'd gotten Alena back, he was ready to exact his revenge on me for putting his daughter in that danger. If he had the same adrenaline buzzing through his veins that I did, he'd probably want to settle this with his fists.

He stopped in front of both of us, the snarl on his face slowly unflinching.

Then suddenly, he unfurled an empty hand, holding it out to me. It looked like he wanted to shake my hand.

I stared at it in shock for a moment. Then I reached out and shook it.

"Thank you for saving Alena. For putting her life above your own," he said stiffly.

"Viktor, I owe you thanks, too, for helping us with our situation. And I owe you an apology for giving you a hard time."

He shrugged, and his eyes went to Sasha. "I don't like you being with someone else, Sasha," he said, his eyes softening. "You will always be my beautiful *solnyshka*."

She let out a slow breath, gazing at him uneasily as he touched her cheek.

"But, if you are going to be happy with someone else, I am glad it is a man who I trust. Who I know will protect you and Alena. That is good," he said.

I saw the relief in Sasha's eyes. Her face brightened and she smiled, even as tears appeared in her eyes. "He will. I know he will," she whispered.

"Yeah, I will," I agreed, gazing at Sasha and stroking her hand in mine. "Always."

"Good," he said, turning to leave. Before he took a step, he added, "Otherwise, I'll kill you."

As he walked outside, Sasha looked up at me and shrugged. "I don't think he was kidding," she said. "He's never joked once in his life."

I pulled her to me. "I don't think he was, either. But it doesn't matter. If anything happens to either of you on my watch, I'll kill myself."

Epilogue

Sasha

"Oh, my God, it looks so good!" I screamed as Grace and I went into the newly painted room in Zain's house.

Our house, now.

Grace gushed, "I love the color!" She turned this way and that, admiring the way the light streamed in through the white shutters and hit the walls. "What is it?"

"It's called 'blue skies'," I said as Zain inched past me with the paint tray and squeezed my side.

"Hey. Get out of here. The fumes."

I rolled my eyes. "That's old paint. New paint is totally safe."

"Oh, so do you mean *you* could've done this?" he said to me with a grin.

"Ha. Ha." I said to him, elbowing his thick bicep. He knew I'd been spending much of my time fixing up his parents' old house and making it into a home. There was plenty of work to be done, since the house was HUGE, and he hadn't done anything to most of the house in years. At first, we'd discussed selling it, but then we decided that it had the perfect yard for kids to run around in, was perfectly located near the schools and everything else we needed in Aveline Bay.

So, we decided to keep it and fix it up.

Zain was proving to be quite the handyman. He'd redone an old room for Alena, completely demolished and renovated the kitchen with a bunch of his brothers. Then, when I'd started to show, he said it was about time he began with the nursery.

Yes, in four months, I'd be having a baby. A baby boy this time.

I caressed my stomach as he leaned forward to kiss me. Then he leaned down farther, laying a kiss on my belly. "How's my little champ doing today?"

"We're all doing fine," I said, rolling my eyes at Grace. I'd been joking to her that Zain asked me that question about a thousand times a day.

Grace and I went downstairs to sit out on the patio, to wait for the other guests to arrive. We were planning on having a big housewarming party today, with all his brothers and our friends, since it was a beautiful day. But of course, Zain was so excited about the nursery that he woke up bright and early that morning to paint it, leaving me with all the prep work.

Didn't matter. Grace, who'd quickly become my best friend, had come over to help, and together, we'd gotten much of the work done. Cait had also come over to help babysit.

That was the way we were in the Cobras. Family. We helped each other out.

The Fury were truly gone, now. It'd been over five months since we'd heard anything about them, so now everything the Cobras had gone through felt like a distant memory. Viktor had spoken well of the Cobras, to his Russian contacts, so everything with them was just fine. I still saw Viktor of course, every time we switched off on visitation, and things were going well on that front. He had a pretty serious girlfriend named Masha, who Alena adored.

I was happy for him. He seemed happier, though I still hadn't gotten a smile out of him. And he was truly making an effort to spend more time with Alena when she was at his place.

"Hi, Mommy!" she called to me from the swing as we went outside. She jumped off and came running to me. Now five, she was an independent bundle of energy, a fashionista, and destined to give her daddy heart palpitations in a few years.

I hugged her. "Go inside and get changed into your pretty dress, okay? People will be arriving soon."

She squealed in delight and ran to the screen door. "Okay, Mommy," she said, whipping it open and letting it smack closed behind her.

Cait came up, holding Ella's hand as she helped her up the stairs. Ella grinned up at me, so I bent down and kissed her nose. "You have fun on the swing set?"

She nodded excitedly.

Zain had insisted on installing a massive wood play set in the backyard. It was amazing. He said he'd had one there while he was growing up. It was Alena's favorite thing in the world.

Grace, Cait, Ella and I sat under an umbrella by the patio, overlooking the yard, drinking lemonade. "This is really a beautiful house," Cait gushed, pulling her knees up to her chest. "I love this old architecture."

"Thank you," I said. "It's so huge, though. But we're working through it, room by room."

"It looks gorgeous," Cait said.

"You'll just have to find some way to fill all those empty bedrooms!" Grace added with a laugh, looking at my swelling belly.

"Did you guys set a date for the wedding?" I asked her. "We're starting to wonder."

Grace nodded. "Yes. July seventh," she said proudly. "Cullen didn't want to move forward with any wedding plans because of the Fury. But now that they're gone, it's all good."

I clapped my hands excitedly. "I'm so excited for you two. I love weddings."

"You two are going to be bridesmaids," Grace said matter-of-factly, as if it was a given. "And of course, Charlotte and Nora and Liv. And all the Cobras will be Cullen's groomsmen. We might do it on a yacht. We thought that would be romantic."

"Wow," I gushed. "Sounds beautiful."

Of course, Cullen, being the son of a famous rock star, had a lot of money to throw around. This would be the wedding of the century, for sure. And to think, a year ago, I'd felt practically alone in this country. Despite getting away from Viktor, I'd had almost no one to depend on.

And now I had a huge family of friends. I'd been welcomed into their group, and now, I felt like I truly belonged. It nearly brought a tear to my eye, every time I thought about it.

"How are things going at work?" Cait asked me, leaning forward and grabbing a pretzel from the snack bowls I'd set out. "Did they say anything about being pregnant?"

I nodded and stroked my belly. I didn't recall being this big this soon with Alena, but now, only five months along, I had a watermelon belly.

I shrugged. "They were happy for me. I'm just going to work until I take maternity leave, and then I might take a year off. I'll go back, though, of course."

Grace raised an eyebrow. "You don't want to be a stay at home mom?"

"No, I mean, I love having kids, but I love my job, too," I explained. "And where I work, they've been a lot more understanding about my family situation."

That had nothing to do with Marina, of course. The new promotion was announced three months ago, and my friend Sarah Chin had been promoted to the administrative supervisor. I couldn't have been happier, because it went to someone truly deserving. Annoyed at being passed over, Marina had made her usual scene and given her notice. After Marina's departure, everything changed. The place was actually positive, and people were helpful and kind. It was true what they say about toxic people, and how one bad apple can spoil the whole bunch.

Anyhow, Sarah was amazing as a supervisor. She was understanding, encouraging, supportive . . . everything I wanted in a boss. Plus, she let me work my own hours, and for the first time, I'd been getting praise from the lawyers, and actually feeling like I was making a difference.

Work wasn't a burden anymore. I loved it.

But most of all, I loved coming home, finding Zain at home with Alena, both of them playing with dolls and laughing their heads off. He'd pick her up sometimes from daycare and the two of them would do all sorts of things together. She loved him like crazy.

"What about you, Cait? How is your mom?" I asked as Drake came up behind her, massaging her shoulders. He was clearly so in love with her, it practically radiated off of him.

"Oh, she's great," she said with a smile. "Has a new boyfriend. Some tax accountant who lives in L.A. I barely ever see her anymore, she's so happy."

"That's great," Grace said. For a while there, the two of them could barely leave the house, since Cait was former Fury president Slade's daughter, and kept on a tight leash. Now that the Fury had been decimated, they were enjoying their freedom. "But what's that on your finger?"

Cait held out her hand, and Drake grinned like the cat who swallowed the canary. "Oh, yes. Drake proposed last night."

We all gasped, and Grace practically lunged across the table to look at the glinting diamond. "Oh, my God! It's gorgeous!"

"Congratulations!" I said, and the rest of the group offered their well wishes.

"What the hell's going on here?" Jet said, appearing at the gate. "I could hear you assholes yelling from all the way down the street."

"We were just celebrating the news. Cait and Drake are engaged."

Jet smirked at his brother and punched him. "Took you long enough."

"Yeah? When are you going to get your ass in gear with Nora?" Drake said, crossing his arms.

He shrugged. "You know me. I ain't all fancy. But if she asks me, I might say yes."

We all rolled our eyes. "But where is Nora?" I asked.

"She's finishing up a shift at the clinic. She'll be here later," he answered as Drake handed him a beer. He took a swig and looked around. "This shithole's really shaping up."

Just then, Zain came out and wrapped an arm around him and Drake. "Hell, Jet. You're as charming as ever." He smacked his head. "What the hell did Nora see in you?"

He shrugged. "My big dick."

We all burst out laughing. Grace gave him a stern look. "Hey. Little big ears, here." She motioned off to Alena, who'd just arrived in her pink dress.

Everyone made a fuss about her showing up. She blushed at first, which was usual around large groups of people, but once she got used to it, she wouldn't shut up. Zain scooped her up and kissed her little cheek. "You look beautiful, Alena. Just as beautiful as your mom."

She giggled, and he met my gaze across the yard. I smiled at him, my heart fluttering just as it always did whenever he was around.

A few moments later, Nix and Liv arrived. I'd always envied how graceful Liv looked, even when nine months pregnant, which was how she was when I met her. She was a ballerina, and carried her pregnancy so well, compared to me. Here I was, five months along, and I felt like a giant whale. Luckily, whenever Zain looked at me, I felt like a princess.

Cait moved out of her chair so that Liv could sit with her five-month old baby, a chubby little boy named Connor. He was so cute, all of us leaned in to play with him as he blew bubbles and giggled. She passed him over to Grace, who bounced him on her knee, making him giggle even louder.

"How are you doing, Liv?" Grace asked.

"Oh. Good. Getting back into shape for dance. Nix and I are looking into a place downtown. Aveline Bay really doesn't have a great dance studio. We're thinking of opening one. For little kids."

Jet laughed. "You going to get your tutu on, big brother?"

Nix pretend-coughed out a "Fuck you" and headed inside with an aluminum-foil covered dish which had to have been Liv's famous potato salad.

Liv smiled at him as he left. "Oh, yes, he's going on pointe soon. He's going to be my best student!"

"Does he know about this?" I asked.

"Oh, here they come! Here they come!" Cait said suddenly, peering down the driveway.

We all waited with our breaths held as Charlotte appeared, holding a car seat. "Hi!" she said in a hushed whisper, bringing up the car seat and setting it down on the table. We all peered in and saw the tiny baby, little Joel, named after her brother, who'd been murdered in cold blood.

"Oh, he's so beautiful," we all cooed, peering at his tiny little baby parts. "He's perfect."

Charlotte beamed. "I was worried, being a couple months premature, that it was going to be tough. But Joel is a fighter."

Behind her, Hart nodded. "He's definitely an ass-kicker. Just about as stubborn as his uncle."

"How are you?" I asked Charlotte as she slid into an open seat. She looked tired, probably from those sleepless nights taking care of a new baby, but happy.

"Oh. Great. I decided I won't be going back to work at the Animal Hospital, at least, not yet. I have enough to handle, with Joel and all the critters at home."

Alena wormed her way through the crowd and crawled onto one of the chairs to look at the baby. "Look but don't touch, okay?" I warned her.

She nodded. "My mommy's having a boy baby, too," she announced proudly to anyone who would listen. "We're going to name him Flynn."

At this news, everyone looked at me. I shrugged. No idea where that name had come from. Probably a movie she'd seen.

Before I could say anything, Zain spoke up. "That's today. She changes every day. Yesterday, she wanted to name him Prince Eric."

I grinned at him. "Zain wants to call him Axle."

He shrugged. "Hey. It's a good name. Tough."

"I don't want tough! I want a sweet little mama's boy who never forgets his mommy."

He scoffed at that. "My son's gonna be riding a motorcycle from the time he's four. His first bike'll be a mini Harley."

The guys all nodded their heads in agreement. I truly didn't put it past him. He spent almost as much time in the garage, working on his bike, as he did in bed with me. Sometimes I felt like his mistress, and the bike, his true love. I'd told him that, once, and he'd said, "Well, I love both of you, but you're a hell of a lot nicer to curl up next to in bed."

After we all fussed over little Joel, we all went inside. As I was setting out the buffet, the crock pot of pulled pork, the potato salad, the rolls, the pickles, baked beans, corn on the cob, macaroni salad, and fruit, Nora walked in, pulling off her jacket and waving at everyone. Jet came up to her and kissed her nose.

We all went outside to eat as the sun began to set and the moon shone over the enormous, quiet backyard. Zain lit candles all around and turned on little fairy lights. He also piped in some smooth jazz, so the mood remained festive and fun.

As I was coming outside with my plate, he wrapped his arms around me from behind and kissed my neck. "Happy?"

I nodded. "So happy. You have no idea."

He nuzzled my neck, smelling me, dragging his lips down to my collarbone. "Good. That's what I like to hear from my pretty lady."

I smiled. That was what he called me the first night we met.

I turned around and looked up at him. He kissed me, then gave me a look that told me everything I needed to know. A look that said he wanted me, needed me, and would protect Alena and me for the rest of his life. That said he was just as happy as I was.

Then I went down to the picnic tables, where all the Cobras and their wives and family were assembled, talking and having fun. People who would constantly have my back, as long as we lived. My American Family. Who knew that growing up outside of Moscow, Russia, I would find everything I wanted and needed in life in a little town called Aveline Bay, California?

I was so lucky, so happy, and so loved.

And best of all, I got to spend the rest of my days with Zain, my bad-ass motorcycle man who'd changed my life for the better, the moment he walked in.

THE END

Acknowledgements

Thank you so much for reading my books! I appreciate you so much. Without you, I couldn't do what I do.

Thanks to KB Winters for dragging me along this journey. And extra special thanks to all my FB fans, ARC readers, editors and everyone who helps me publish my books. You know who you are and I love you for it.

Thank you!

Evie

About The Author

I love fairytales, princesses and bad boys. I just didn't realize how much until I started writing about them. I have found a new love in my life and I hope you have too!

You can find all of my books at EvieMonroe.com

facebook.com/eviemonroeauthor/

eviemonroeauthor@gmail.com

eveimonroe.com

Made in the USA
Coppell, TX
18 February 2023

13033682R00236